Normal as we Are

Author Desraye Halon

This book is dedicated to D. M. J.

Without you, this book would not have been possible.

Thank you for everything, you will always be in our hearts.

Printed in the United States of America

ISBN 978-1-312-42767-9

Normal as we Are

Author Desraye Halon

First Printing, 2014

Created 2008

RyBlu Publishing – Phoenix , AZ

Editing by D. S. C.

Photography for cover by Terese Halon
Azad

Normal as we Are

Chapter 1

Sun soaked afternoon field, wind lightly blowing through the tall grass. The swaying back and fourth of the drying weeds, it almost sounds like someone whispering softly into your ear. Pine, oak, maple, just some of the huge trees that can be seen for miles. Locus buzzing their wings as they fly along a stretch of gravel and dirt driveway. Twisting and turning as if there is no end.

A beautiful two-story farmhouse sits at the end of the old road and the twisting long driveway. Pretty yellow and purple flowers fill the boxes around the well-kept front porch. Clothes hanging on the line out back to dry makes a whipping noise as the wind blows through their crisp fabric. Something you might see in a magazine on someone's coffee table for show. A big red barn sits far back on the 30-acre property; no animals, just some tools and a tractor find their home inside of it. Next to a small pond with some Sunfish and turtles in it lined with cattails and medium smooth rocks. Quiet and peaceful, all too relaxing on a summer day. Like you are driving up to a dream or a little piece of America that has been kept in a glass globe just for you to look at.

A dark SUV that is a few years older sits in the driveway in front of the farmhouse. A tall thin woman with long brown hair, with a couple of piercings in her lip and in her eyebrow is getting into the driver's seat. Another young woman peaks her head out the door of the house and yells out to the SUV, "Don't forget to bring me home some smokes on your way back from work. All right?" The horn sounds and the vehicle backs up and starts down the long winding gravel drive to the main road. Rock music plays as a beautiful young woman is checking her makeup in the rearview mirror. "Tara, you are looking good bitch." She says to herself out loud.

Tara is heading into Portland, where she works as a bartender at a small dirty bar, dimly lit and there is tape on some of the bar stools. It's a place where a lot of the locals like to hang out after work. Mostly men and some of the tired old looking women in town looking for that right man to take back to their small run down trailer. The rum and coke type of women, with the raspy voice from years of smoking that make you cringe at the mere sight of them setting at the end of the bar. The sun is starting to set and neon city lights take over the sky in the distance. This place is off the beaten path.

Tara arrives at the bar to start her shift. The owner Lou, a short balding man smelling of cigar smoke and bad aftershave and a waitress are sitting at the bar getting ready for the bar to open as she walks through the dark sticker clad doorway. “Hey Tara, see the news today?” Asks owner Lou. “Yea. Messed up isn’t it? Four girls missing now they said.” Tara replies. Lou says, “I don’t want anyone leaving tonight alone.” “Yea yea” said the waitress. “Got it Lou!”

Across town there is a woman, Michelle, but she goes by Mitch, she is in her late 30’s, she is calling it a night from work. She always carries a knife and a handgun. Ex-navy, now working for a security contractor that goes all over the world whenever they are needed to help out the U.S. government. Bringing in food or supplies for the troops. She is hardcore, in shape, attractive but a bit worn, hardly ever cracks a smile. She heads out to the bar for a drink to relax. She walks through the door and walks past a handful of people over to the end of the bar and sits down. “Hey Mitch” says Tara, “I’ll have a scotch on the rocks." Mitch says. "Did ya hear about all those girls going missing?" Tara says to Mitch. "Yes, you just never know. This world is going insane sometimes I think. It's funny how one girl goes missing and it's nothing, no one even cares, but a few disappear then people start to notice, like one isn't enough?" says Mitch. "You getting off work soon?" Mitch asks Tara. "No, not for a while." says Tara. "Be careful then, and watch yourself." says Mitch. "Yeah, thanks. You too Mitch." "I'm out of here Tara, see ya on the flip side. Later." Says Mitch. Lou just watches Mitch as she walks out of the bar then looks at Tara as he puffs from his cigar.

On her way home Mitch sees a girl walking on the side of a dark desolate road where there are only a few streetlights every few miles for light. She slows down and yells out her car window for the girl to be careful, then offers her a ride but the girl turned it down. The girl tells Mitch to mind her own business. So Mitch drives off down the road to home without another thought about her. Headlights hit the gravel drive; Mitch slowly drives the winding driveway up to the farmhouse. She turns off the engine, walks in the door, she's home. A voice yells out, "Did you get my smokes?" "You need to quit." said Mitch. A small-framed well-kept blonde haired bubbly girl named Christa comes dancing down the stairs listening to her MP3 playing softly, circling around Mitch and poking at her sides. "Come on sweetie, lighten up." she says to Mitch. "I thought you were Tara, she's going to bring me some cigarettes home. I've been cleaning all day, to keep my mind off of not having a damn cigarette, I'm freaking ready to crack!" Christa tells Mitch.

Candlelight illuminates the rooms of the overly clean farmhouse. Books on the shelves are in alphabetical order by subject not author. Scent of potpourri and lemon collide with a pleasant scent of fresh air slightly blowing in past the curtains throughout the farmhouse. Pillows on the sofa are all at a perfect slight angle. No dust to be seen anywhere, not even on the picture frames on the walls. "I see headlights coming up the drive. Tara's home!" Christa exclaims. "Thank God for that, you were starting to make me want to kick your ass." Mitch grumbled under her breath. Tara walks in and throws a carton of cigarettes at Christa, and tells her about the missing girls that she read about in today's paper. Christa asks, "What did the paper say about it, they have any leads or anything?" Mitch replies, "Just that they're all from the same area, less than a mile apart." "Huh, I guess that is really close together isn't it." Christa says. "That's an understatement." says Tara. "The F.B.I.'s involved in it now too. They think it is someone that knows all of them because it's so close together to each other. No suspects or anything, just like they disappeared into thin air. It's freaking out the people in town though, that's all anyone at the bar can talk about. How about you Mitch? You're in the biz, what's the word?" Tara asked Mitch. "Same shit, nobody knows anything, just a lot more missing people over the last few years in the surrounding states but nothing this close together. We have an inside guy in the F.B.I., but I'm not sure if he would even say anything about it to us. Need-to-know bases I guess. I'll feel him out about it; he has been wanting to get together for a while to catch up over lunch or something. I guess I can give him a call tomorrow and set up a time. Other than that I'm tired of talking about it right now, I don't want to be bringing the office home unless I absolutely have to. I work long enough hours as it is." said Mitch. Tara speaks, "I'm going to my room to try and sleep, don't forget to lock the windows before you go to bed Christa." "Don't worry, I'm on top of it mom!" says Christa to Tara. "Ha ha ha, smart ass, good night you two." The sounds of crickets chirp in the night back ground and Tara's footsteps fades as she walks upstairs to her bedroom.

Christa lights up a cigarette and grabs an ice water out of the fridge and goes into the family room toward the back of the house where the computer is kept. She signs on to the Internet to surf the web where she usually can be found until the early morning hours. Mitch stares blankly out the window into the night world as she sips on a small glass of scotch and wonders about what the town's people really think about the girls that have gone missing and do they really care in the big scheme of things. Prices of gas and food climbing and jobs becoming scarce, people can't feed their families, maybe it would be a blessing in a strange way for some people if they had their whole family go missing. She heads to her bedroom after she finished her scotch with her wondering thoughts.

Chapter 2

The morning sun shines in past the curtains through the windows. Tara walks slowly down the stairs to the kitchen. Smell of fresh coffee fills the house. “I made coffee for you bitches!” exclaims Christa. “Christa, don’t you ever get tired of that? I couldn’t stay up all night on the computer and be a happy ass whore like you are all the damn time, you know there are only whack jobs on line right?" Tara said. "That's what I love about it, all the wana be freaks! I'm trying to stay connected with the people!" stated Christa. "Well it's going to be a busy day for us I have a few errands to run, pay some bills, then maybe some yard work I guess. Work, work, work, then play, play, play!" Tara said. Christa went upstairs to wake Mitch up, and take a short nap for a few hours to get refreshed for some chores and the evenings events of fun they have planned.

As they, and everyone else gets around to start their day in the world around them, there is a faint sound of gasping combined with shallow muffled cries rising into the air for no one to hear. The gasps are coming from a young woman with medium light brown hair and a small frame, pretty, with smooth clear milky skin in her early twenties. Clanging of chains against cement make echoes through the space. Even with eyes wide open she can't see anything through the thick darkness that is her hell, she can only feel the coldness of the brick and the floor, only hearing the chains and her own muffled sounds. The chains bind her arms behind her back to a brick wall, only giving her inches to move around. It's damp and musty. She tries to remain calm, but her mind is racing, she doesn't even know if this is real or just a horrible nightmare, and if so, she just wants to wake up from it. Trying to retrace her thoughts of what happened to her, it's just so foggy in her mind. She slightly remembers walking to the corner store but she just can't remember how far she got or anything that happened. She feels numbness down by her hips and legs, a very uncomfortable weird feeling in her lower abdomen. All of the sudden she hears a light thud, it sounds like it's coming from the right side of her small area of hell. (Thunk thunk!) There it is again, that sound. She becomes very still, trying to hear what and where this noise is coming from within the dark. She can hear moaning and groaning, like if someone is trying to yell out, but can't. She thinks maybe like her, someone else is there, bound and gagged like she is. Tears roll down her face mixing with her sweat, as she is stricken with panic and unknown fear, a fear she has never felt in her life. The young woman cannot even whisper out to anyone there, her mouth is gagged with a towel and tape over it, making her breath in and out harder and harder through her nose as her fear inside her moves to a new level she has never felt or even thought about. She thinks maybe its better that it is so dark she cannot see anything. Fearing there are more women where she is in the darkness, like her. She wonders in horror if this is some kind of human trafficking that she has seen on the news. Selling young pretty girls for sex or some sort of slavery to work for free in a distant country far from her clean comfy home life in the Pacific North West.

Tara is off driving down the road to town to get her chores and errands done. Music blaring on the radio, Tara is singing along to some heavy metal music, thinking about her tasks at hand. First the liquor store, then grocery store, and last the gas station. Tara pulls up to the liquor store and gets out of her truck with the music still stuck in her head she goes to walk into the store and a man grabs her arm from behind. She turns around and sees this big fat Billy Bob type just grinning and looking at her. “What the hell you back woods freak! Get your damn nasty hand off me before I cut your balls off!” Tara yells at the man. Another man runs out of the store and up to them and grabs the Billy Bob man off her. “I’m really sorry miss, this is my brother, and he doesn’t mean any harm. Sometimes he just gets excited around people, he’s a bit slow. Please accept my apologies Miss.” the man says to Tara. “Well maybe you should keep your brother on a fucking small leash. Freak!” Tara yell out. “You don’t have to be a bitch about it.” the man said back to her in a nasty tone. About that time the Sheriff was driving by and saw what was going on and pulled into the parking lot to see what was happening. “Hey Tara, any trouble here?" the Sheriff asked. "No, no trouble, just the freak off the leash here with his brother not being able to keep his hands off women I guess." Tara told the Sheriff. "Hey my brother is no freak, he just doesn't get out much. He wouldn't hurt anybody Sheriff." the man explained to the Sheriff. "Well, let's all just move it along here. Take him home and calm him down so there's no trouble here." said the Sheriff. Tara thanked the Sheriff for stopping and remarked that maybe he should keep an eye on him with all those girls that have gone missing lately. The Sheriff said, "I don't think he's the one but maybe I will keep an eye on him if there's any more trouble that comes about from him." "Yeah, thanks Sheriff. See ya up at the bar when I work again." Tara said as she winks at the Sheriff and blows him a kiss while she walked into the store to finish up her list of things to do to so she can get home and relax.

Tara is finally done with all her running around and, at last, comes pulling down the road to the house and sees the yard work has already been finished up. “Thank ya Jesus!” Tara exclaimed. Christa meets Tara outside to help her bring in all the groceries and other things she had gotten. “I’m soooo glad you two got the yard work done! Now we can just party a little tonight.” Tara said. “Where’s Mitch?” asks Tara. Christa replies, “Oh speaking of Mitch, She told me she likes you, like has the hots for you Tara.” Tara turns her head away from Christa so she won’t see her trying to hide a smile. Tara replies, “Oh really? She told you that? Mitch just blurted it out to you, ‘Hey Christa, I really like Tara she’s just so freaking hot!” “Christa answers,

"Well, not quite like that but she did mention it to me. I think it's great! I have always thought you two should hook up." Tara says, "Well I guess tonight will be extra interesting and more exciting than normal. We better get this party started soon and stop talking so much bullshit. Let the games begin!" They both go in and unpack the bags of food and alcohol. Putting everything in its place, all labels facing forward in the cabinets and fridge. Nothing is ever out of its place; even the towels that hang in the kitchen are always even and folded neatly.

Mitch walks in to the room. "Hey, I almost forgot to tell you guys. I was going into the damn store and this weird guy with his brother grabbed me. Nothing big, nothing to worry about, but the Sheriff pulls up and sees this guy grab me. So I tell him, 'you better watch out for that guy with all these young girls going missing lately.' The Sheriff is like, oh yeah maybe you're right. What a freak. Now the cops will be looking at that slow guy and his brother. I just think it's so damn funny!" Tara exclaims. They all look at each other and just bust out laughing about it. "I'm going to laugh about that all night Tara, you're so stupid!" Christa says while laughing. "Well, on that note, I'm going to go roll a few joints and light some candles for this evening". Christa says as she walks out of the room.

Chapter 3

Back in the dank darkness of hell, the young woman can hear music that started playing softly, not loud enough to make out what the song is, but loud enough to know there is music and must be some people close by. She tries to remain calm but she just can't, knowing that someone is near. All those horrible thoughts came rushing back into her head about the sex slave news reports she has seen on television. Her heart is racing; it feels like it will just jump right out of her chest or her throat. She just wants to get out, get away and run home, run anywhere and hide. All the thoughts of the unknown make her sick to her stomach, she needs to stay calm though. She doesn't want to make herself vomit with the gag in her mouth. Just then she hears the thumping on the wall again. She becomes very still and listens. Maybe she will hear someone talking or something about what it is or what will happen to her. But all she can hear is the thumping on the wall and her own breathing just echoes louder and louder. Her breathing just gets faster and faster and the heat in the room is too much for her. Her mind spins out of control and she passes out in the dark airless room.

Back in town the Sheriff is thinking about what happened at the store earlier today with Tara and the mentally slow man. The Sheriff knows the brother of the mentally slow man somewhat but doesn't ever remember him mentioning about him having a brother, mentally slow or not. He makes a few calls about it to his deputies and has them out asking people about him and checking it out around the town.

The Sheriff looks down at his desk and sees a missing girl's flyer for the last young woman to go missing. He studies it, just staring at the flyer looking at her medium light brown hair, her perfect skin and trying to reach into her eyes for any clues, signs, or anything at all. She never got into any trouble, didn't have friends with questionable backgrounds either. She graduated high school with good grades and started working at the local dollar store trying to save money to better herself so she could one day be able to go to college. The Sheriff just couldn't figure it out. All the young women who went missing were the same in age and race but that's about it, different backgrounds, educations, and friends. They didn't know each other. Where they went missing from and the times of day were just all too very random. He just couldn't find any other connection, other than their ages, all of them are in their early twenties and Caucasian.

He just knows it isn't going to turn out well, with four young women missing and them not being found yet. No bodies, no anything turning up about them and the girls all living so close together in this area. Like a spaceship came down and just sucked them up into the sky without warning or cause.

One of the deputies came back to the station to report what he found out about the man and his mentally ill brother. "Well what's the story out there Frank?" asked the Sheriff. Frank replied, "Nothing, it all checks out. He just had his brother move out here from California. His brother's name is James Lee Brunk, mentally retarded. He has the mind of a nine year old, his sister couldn't take care of him anymore and they didn't want to put him in a home. She said it's just too much work between him, her 3 kids and a full time job. That's why she had him move out here, to live with her other brother, Phil. Phil doesn't have any kids or a wife and he owns his own heating and cooling business. No criminal record of any kind. I even called the school for special education for adults he was going to in California and talked to the Dean of Students. Nothing, said he was a good guy always helping out around the school. Did well in his programs. If you ask me Sheriff I don't think he has anything to do with those girls going missing. Him grabbing Tara today, I think that was just a fluke. He didn't hurt her or anything, so you got me. But I think they're in the clear." "Thanks Frank, I'm glad you followed through and got back to me so fast." said the Sheriff. "You bet! You're the boss Sheriff." said Frank.

The Sheriff wonders if the F.B.I. is telling him all the information that they have receive over the last few weeks. He ponders it for a while as he looks through all the information, photos, and statements made in these cases so far. Not finding anything new jumping out at him about the young women. He decided to place a call to the F.B.I., but he knows it might not get him anywhere, after all he is only a Sheriff in a small town and not privileged to the other government agencies information unless it is given.

The Sheriff places the call (ring ring), "Hello Agent Woodman speaking, what can I do for you?" The F.B.I. agent says as he answers the phone. "This is Sheriff James Kindel in Prescott County, OR. I wanted to see if I could get an update or any more information about the missing young women out here please?" Agent Woodman replies, "No, not a thing in yet, we'll let you know if anything new would help you out, but until then you just keep working the people in town for us and let us know if anything comes up, okay Sheriff. Sheriff Kindel isn't it?" "Yes, Sheriff James Kindel is my name like I said before." Answers the Sheriff. Agent Woodman cuts in over the Sheriff's voice on the phone. "Like I said, we'll let you know. We're real busy here Sheriff, I'll call you if I need to tell you anything new on the case, Goodbye." Before the Sheriff could say anymore he heard a click and silence from the other end. "Son of a bitch! They think they're so damn important over there!" yelled the Sheriff. He just shakes his head in disgust and with his teeth clinched tightly together he slowly walks out of the station for the night. He gets in his truck and heads for home, where he can at least talk to someone who really appreciates him, his dog.

Chapter 4

Fire gently dances on candles burning from the patio table with music playing as Mitch gets the grill ready for the New York Strip steaks to be cooked for their evening party. Whenever the three women have a night off from work together they like to prepare a nice dinner with drinks and just cut loose to unwind from their lives. A chance to get all caught up with each other's issues and or problems. Especially Mitch enjoys this time together to relax and forget about her high stress job working with all the different government agencies. She did worry about tonight somewhat because Christa told Tara that Mitch liked her, a lot! They are all close friends and didn't want it to be weird or different even though they are all aware of their sexuality, she didn't want any strain on the close friendship they all had. Christa and Mitch have fucked a few times over the years but they try to keep it friendlier or just fuck buddies that no one knows about so it doesn't get complicated. Tara doesn't even know that the two have fucked on and off over the years. Mitch has been avoiding Tara most of the day just trying to think of the right way to just come out and say it. Mitch isn't shy at all; she just doesn't express her feelings like other people. She usually keeps everything to herself not wanting anyone to ever think of her as weak, whether mentally or physically. "Hi Mitch." Tara says happily to Mitch with a half-cocked smile as her eyes peak through her long bangs as she walks out onto the patio to pour some drinks for all of them. "Hey Tara, I'll have a scotch on the rocks." "Of course you will, I swear I don't think I've ever seen you drink anything else." said Tara. Mitch replies, "Tara, I'm going to say something to you, so just let me say it without any interruptions. I'm sure you have heard from big mouth Christa that I like you. I have feelings for you, but it's not a problem if you don't feel anything back. But I am asking you if you'd like to go out on a date or something. So, what do you think?" Tara lets out a soft gentle laugh with a great smile. Mitch's heart starts to pound in anticipation of Tara's answer. Tara explains to Mitch. "You're so romantic Mitch, what a way to ask a girl out. Well it seems we already know each other all too well, so it makes sense to be drawn to each other. You're very sexy, smart and funny in your own dry way. (A short but painful pause) I think it would be a good idea to explore these feelings. I'm feeling it too, sexy." Tara walks up to Mitch and runs a few fingers through her hair then leans in for a passionate but small kiss, then pulls away and smiles at Mitch. Tara says, "I'm sure Christa will get off on this new development, don't you think?" All of the sudden there is a loud bang! They both jump with hearts racing and look around. What the hell was that shit!"

exclaims Tara. Everything is quite as they look around to see what and where the noise came from. Out jumps Christa from under the table on the patio. “Hey freaks! You were getting a little too serious for me.” she said as she was laughing uncontrollably. It was a firecracker she threw from under the table, while she was ease dropping on them. “You’re a jackass Christa!” yelled Tara. Then they all just looked at each other and started laughing lightly hitting each other. “I love you guys, you’re so easy.” said Christa.

The steaks went on the grill as the girls are talking over drinks. Chatting about their week and what they hated about their jobs and how they would like to change lives with different people around the world. Except

Christa, she doesn't work, she just stays at home and cleans, cooks and smokes weed, so she doesn't have a lot of issues. They watched the sun go down on the day as they finished their candlelit dinner together. "Well, I guess it's time to clean this mess up so we can get on to the REAL PARTY!" Tara said. "Yeah, I know I have been looking forward to tonight all week long." Mitch said. "Hey if you two want to finish up the cleaning out here I'll go get the other stuff ready for us?" asked Christa." "Oh, yes please do", replied Tara. "Well, I'm off then. See you two in a few minutes."

Chapter 5

Christa walks downstairs to the basement, nicely done with carpet and a pool table. There is a bookshelf on the far wall, she pushes it in toward the wall slightly, and it clicks. She pulls the bookshelf away from her. It's a hidden doorway that opens up to a slightly musky hallway with three metal doors on one side and two on the other. The first room she comes to is a storage room, a few rows of metal shelves filled with garden tools, surgical tools, plastic liners, cleaner and the like. Another room has a shower, but no shower curtain. The whole room is covered in plastic and there's a big metal sink. There is also a metal shelf affixed to the wall, on the shelf are some surgical masks, gowns, and gloves.

Christa pulls her hair back into a ponytail and puts on a gown, mask and gloves. She then goes over to a door on the other side and opens it, the sound of a metal lock echoes through the hallway loudly. Light blasts into the room, so bright it almost blinded the girl chained to the wall. She can't see because she has been in total darkness for days. All the girl can make out is a dark shadow standing in the doorway with the light blaring in from behind the shadow. The girl doesn't know what is happening, she starts to moan through the gag in her mouth and tears roll down her pretty face under her dirty hair. She is weak from not eating for about three days. "Oh man, look. You peed on yourself." Christa leaves the door open and walks back to the other room for a pair of scissors then walks back into to the room and starts to cut off the young woman's pants and panties. Christa then walks to the corner of the room and grabs a hose and turns it on, she hoses her down with cold water for a few minutes. The young woman moans out as loudly as she can, the icy cold water is a shock to her body, the girl starts to cry and moan in a panic. "There you go, clean enough. At least you don't smell like piss any more, dirty girl." Christa say as she laughs right in the girls face.

The other girls come down to the basement and both put on a gown, mask and gloves. Christa unchains her cold shivering body from the wall. The girl can't even fight back as she is too weak and confused. Mitch walks over and grabs her under her arms, Christa grabs the girl by her ankles and they put her on a cold metal embalming table they have set up in the room which the girl never saw in the darkness. As Mitch and Christa hold her weak body down, Tara places the girl's wrists and ankles in restraints attached to the embalming table. The girl tries to scream out but still has the gag in her mouth so she just makes moans with muffed shrieks as she tries to wiggle around on the table with her eyes wide open in fear, tears are mixing with sweat and just running down the sides of her face as she lies there. Tara then places a restraint over her forehead and one across her hips so the girl will remain still for them. The girl can't believe what she is seeing, just three people in masks and gloves, she can't see anything but their eyes, she has no idea who they are but can tell they are all women, and she just can't believe it. Tara turns on a radio softly, not too loud, on some rock n roll station. Christa grabs some surgical tools, scalpel, retractors and clamps. Then she grabs some regular tools, pliers, garden shears and a jig saw then places them on a small stand next to the table. Mitch takes the scalpel in hand, looks the girl in the eyes and says "This is really going to hurt dear." Mitch tells her as she places the scalpel on her flesh on the left side of her chest over her heart and slowly presses the blade down cutting her open about eight inches long and then downward. The girl is violently moving about and trying to scream out for her life, but no one that can help her will ever hear her shrill cries. Christa places a retractor in the cut to hold it open, Mitch cuts through the fascia and muscle, the retractors are replaced to hold that back as they slowly cut into her without any pain medication of any kind. Revealed are her ribs on the left side, Mitch then takes a pair of small garden shears and snips away at the girls ribs to get to her still beating heart in her chest. Tara slowly pets the girl's legs moving up to her pussy, just slowly and softly petting her as Mitch carefully cuts the thin sac around her heart after enough ribs have been removed to get her hand inside. Mitch reaches in and caresses the girl's heart, feeling it beat in her hand; Mitch closes her eyes and feels the deep power and total control within her hand now. With her other hand she runs her fingers through the girls hair while looking deep into her eyes. Mitch squeezes down on her heart until it stops beating, watching the life slowly fade from the girls face. The girl's body shakes for a few seconds then goes limp; eyes wide open, and still some left over tears drip down the side of her lifeless face. "I thought you were going to try to keep this one alive longer? What the fuck Mitch!" Christa screams to Mitch. Mitch replies, "I just can't help myself sometimes, not when it comes to matters of the heart. Sorry. I'll try more self-restraint next time." Christa replies in an annoyed tone, "I was just getting ready to finger fuck her pussy while you worked."

"Well next time is now! We have another girl in there for us. Sounds like a great idea to me." Tara says as she smiles under her mask. They place a couple small towels in the dead girl's chest so blood doesn't get all over the place. They unstrap the dead girl's body and carry it over to the corner of the floor, her back to the corner of the wall so the next girl they are getting ready to bring in can see her already cut open chest stuffed with towels.

All three ladies walk over to another metal door in the hallway, the same loud metal clanking as they turn the lock and open the door unto nothing but darkness. Just like the girl before, the light coming in from the door is blinding, this girl has been locked in this room for three days longer then the girl they just killed. Being locked away for seven days in the darkness, cold and being alone has taken its toll on her mind and her body. She was given two bottles of water and some crackers over the last seven days, but nothing else. She is chained to the wall but has no gag or nothing coving her mouth. She doesn't try and scream, she only tries to cover her eyes to see the shadows that walk through the door with her one free hand, she only has one hand chained to the wall so she could eat and drink over the week. They unchained her arm and walk her over to the room with the shower, they sit her down in an old plastic shower chair you see in a hospital. They turn on the shower for her and let it run warm and the warm water feels nice on her cold dirty body, not cold like the hose water. Mitch watches as the other two ladies wash the girl, one washing her hair and the other washing her body up. The girl is too weak to fight, she can barely hold herself up in the chair as the water rushes over her thin frail body. The girl's body just sways back in fourth in the chair as their hands run through her hair and over her rail thin body, she just keeps her eyes closed as the water hits her face. She drifts off into a vision of a mountain peak after hiking up to the top and looking at all the beauty down below, just as she is getting into a deep thought of a happier place, she is snapped up to her feet and feels hands begin to touch her pussy slowly as one of the ladies wash her. The girl opens her eyes and tries to struggle but only ends up being more like a rage doll with arms trying to push them off of her. As her eyes glance over them and over to Mitch just standing there watching, she can't seem to get her head to wrap around these three people all covered in light blue gowns, gloves, white masks and caps on. The room starts to slowly spin with visions of these people and the white cold brick walls around her, she wonders is she dead, dreaming or maybe she took something she wouldn't have normally taken making her see crazy visions. The girl drops like a bag of sand to the wet hard cement floor, the girls turn off the water and slightly dry her off as she lay there on the floor.

Mitch picks up the small framed girl of barely 110 pounds and carries her over to the first room and places her in a padded chair with wooden arms all covered in a thick see through plastic, there are only wrist restraints hooked to the chair on the arms. Mitch places the old but well-conditioned leather restraints around her wrists and secures the silver buckle tightly in case she awakens again so she can't just jump up if she is able too, which she probably wouldn't be able to if she tried. Tara tells Mitch to start an intravenous line in her left hand to get the girl hydrated. The girl is so weak from lack of food and water they want to make sure she can withstand what they are about to do to her and not just slip into shock when they start to play and torture her. The line is started and Tara squeezes the IV bag to get the solution in her body faster, the IV drip is opened up all the way. The ladies are all wet so they take off their gowns and gloves but keep on their masks for right now, music is playing in the back ground in the small room. Mitch wants the girl to look a little prettier like when they took her, so she has Christa put make up on her face. Foundation is placed on her soft skin, then she carefully puts eye liner on the bottom eyelid, holding the eye lid open slightly as she does. Then a little eyeliner on the top of the lid along the bottom by her eye lashes. A nice rich dark red color of lipstick is placed upon her small lips. Christa combs her wet but drying long blond hair back, then helping it a bit to fall to the sides of her head and face. Just enough make up to bring out the beauty on the young innocent looking girl they had taken.

Although she looks innocent, Mitch never thinks anyone is innocent, she thinks of most, if not all humans, as stupid bumbling prey who cannot be trusted or think for themselves. Humans that just aimlessly wonder through life like zombies, picking over the picturesque landscape and killing other animals on this earth for their own comforts and to ease their fears that they are the kings and queens of this land far and wide. Mitch feels in her own heart that she is doing a service by killing and punishing these vile creatures called humans.

They turn the chair to face the dead girl's body in the corner of the room on the floor, a loud scraping sound fills the room as they turn the chair on the cement floor. Propped up against the wall naked with bloody towels stuffed in her chest, eyes wide open, dried drops of blood splattered across her everywhere and just a look of hopelessness that was left on her face as she died during their game. The IV bag is replaced with another one, as the IV drips quickly in through the needle in her hand, the ladies re-gown and glove up. Mitch walks slowly over to her and just stares at the girl for a few moments, then gets closer to the girls face and kisses her softly on her cheek, then whispers in her ear.

“It’s time to wake up.” The girl doesn’t move at all, Mitch stands up looks at her then kicks the chair and yells as loud as she can in the girls face, “It’s time to wake the fuck up bitch!” The yelling and the shock of the chair being jolted wakes the girl right up back into her hell, her eyes burst open and franticly start searching the room in a panic, her breathing starts to rise to short but deep sporadic bursts, she tries to jump up out of the chair, but she can’t even budge from the restraints. Her legs flail about kicking violently hitting the floor and the legs of the chair, just trying to get up and get away as she looks at the dead girl in the corner. The heel of her foot hits the chair leg so hard you can hear a loud crack, the heel of her foot has broken along with the chair leg splitting but not breaking completely. She doesn’t even feel the pain due to her panicked frenzy that she is in and her brain can't process everything going on around her in this strange world happening right in front of her.

Mitch grabs a pair of medium pliers and a small hard rubber wedge and places the rubber wedge in her mouth on one side in between her teeth. Christa and Tara hold the girls head still as best as they can as Mitch goes in with the pliers and grabs a tooth tightly, but not too tightly as not to crack the tooth. Mitch rocks the tooth back and forth in her mouth with the pliers, it loosens some, and she pulls on the tooth and then rips it from her gums. The girl tries to move her head while screaming out in pain, blood fills her mouth from the missing tooth. Mitch holds the bloody long rooted tooth with the pliers and just looks at it for a few seconds then places it carefully in a small plastic bowl sitting on the little metal table with the tools placed on it neatly. Mitch gets close to the girls face and looks into her eyes and tells her, “Just think, that was just one tooth I pulled, are you ready to be fucked and dismembered?” Mitch has a huge smile. Tears just flow down the girl’s face, black eyeliner running down her cheeks to her neck, she is gagging on the rubber wedge and blood in her mouth as she cries. The girl looks at them, only seeing their eyes over their masks and tries to mumble the words over the wedge and through the blood, “Just kill me, and just kill me fast!” Mitch replies, “I think this is going to work, let’s start by taking one part at a time on this one.” The girl can’t believe what she is hearing, no no no she cries out as tears, bloody spit and snot run down her face as she screams and tries to break loose frantically with the last bit of energy she has left in her beaten body.

Mitch then picks up a butcher knife and a wooden board, Tara places and holds the wooden board under the girl's left hand, using the arm on the chair to help hold it steady. Mitch takes a fast hard swing down at the board and cuts the girl's thumb right off her hand like butter or a knife chopping a carrot in half on a cutting board. Tara pulls the board away; blood just runs out of the area on her hand where her thumb was, dripping quickly onto the cement floor and down the chair making a small pool of blood. Christa hands Mitch a small wood burner, Mitch touches the area around where her thumb was and uses it to cauterize the area to stop the bleeding. It's not a medical tool but it is effective. "There you go sweetie, a brand new look for your hand." Mitch says with a half-smile. As she tries to scream out even more, Mitch stuffs a towel in the girl's mouth. "You might need that to bite down on, see I'm not all bad." Mitch tells the girl as she strokes her hair gently. The girl is trying to scream and cry at the top of her lungs but can't with the towel in her mouth, all you can hear is loud breaths in and out and whimpering coming from her as her face and eyes are bright red. She's all sweaty and just has a look of utmost fear on her face, as if she has just seen the gateway to hell. Mitch starts to hum and doesn't even realize it as she places the wood burner on the girl's chest and writes out the word "whore" across her upper chest just above her breasts. You can hear loud moans, and cries from the girl as tears and snot just run down her face, trying to intake air through her nose only as she's crying frantically and shaking in the chair, still trying to pull her arms away from the chair with everything she has left in her to escape. After a few minutes the girl knows there is just no way out of this, she drops her head down and tries to accept her fate and just hopes for death now. "Well, I think we should keep her for a while, let's clean her wounds up a little and put her back for safe keeping for a few days." Mitch says to the other ladies. The ladies agree and start to clean and wrap her hand up with gauze loosely, then pour some rubbing alcohol on her chest area over the words "whore". As the rubbing alcohol hits her skin she screams out and starts to flail around again in the chair, the burning and stinging of the rubbing alcohol is excruciating, she can feel the pain shoot through every inch of her flesh like razor blades cutting their way out of her.

They undo the wrist restraints and Tara and Christa grab her under her arms and drag her back into the small room down the hall. They sit her down and only put one chain on her ankle so she can move about a little bit in the room. Christa and Tara hold her arms and shoulders down as Mitch walks in to the room with a screwdriver. Mitch grabs the screwdriver by the shaft and holds it in front of her pussy with her hand, like it's her very own cock. Then she places the handle of the screwdriver in the woman's pussy and starts to fuck her hard. As the girls hold her down, she screams for her life and for them to please just stop. Mitch keeps fucking her on the hard cold cement floor as the other two women yell with glee to fuck her good.

After much time has gone by and Mitch is done raping her, they flip the woman over and Mitch rams the handle in her ass a few times for good measure. The woman has been through so much at this point only a few whimpers are heard coming from her as they leave her face down on the floor and torn to shreds inside and out. Just a shivering bloody mass of flesh lay there on the floor now instead of the young beautiful woman of just a week ago.

"You're a good sport, I'll give you some water to drink." Tara says to the girl. Tara gives the girl two bottles of water and some cookies and pours a little bit of whiskey into an empty water bottle to ease her suffering. "Rest well sweetie." Tara says as she shuts the metal door behind her, she does leave the light on in the room for her. As the door closes, the girl yells out to them, “Fucking psycho bitches!” Then just collapses face down on the floor without another sound and just lies there in pain wondering how she will ever escape this madness. The woman can’t believe she is still alive and just wishes for death quickly. She prays to God that he will take her soul and end this horrible life, anything just to end this pain she thought she would never know.

Chapter 6

Tara sighs. "Well, I guess we have to clean up this mess now." Christa pulls her mask and gown off and lights up a joint and says. "It's not like she is going anywhere, let's enjoy the rush." Then Christa takes a long drag off the joint, and exhales with a calmness. Christa turns up the music a bit to help her get in the mood to clean as she smokes. They pick up the dead girl from the corner and place her on the table. Tara starts running water slowly over the girl's limp lifeless body with a garden hose to get the blood running down the drain a bit faster, she doesn't say a word, just looks blankly at the girl's body. Mitch looks at Tara and can see that crushing that girl's heart so fast in the first girl has bummed out Tara and just made her sad. Mitch walks over to Tara and places her hands on Tara's shoulders. "I'm sorry Tara, I really am. I'll make it up to you." Mitch whispers to Tara. Tara replies quickly with a fake smile on her face, "It's ok Mitch, don't worry about it." Then Tara does a short forced laugh and just keeps rinsing the girl's body off until all the blood has gone down the drain. Mitch takes her latex gloves off and throws them in the trash with haste, then she starts grabbing at the bloody used tools on the small table, and tosses them into a deep metal wash sink. She rinses them off watching the blood go down the drain and the remaining flesh clings to the metal on the sink and tools, she has no expression on her face, and a blank stare is all that is there. Just her index finger on her left hand is lightly tapping the metal sink to the beat of the music. She then takes a small soft brush to the tools to get the flesh and blood off of them. "Ok, all rinsed down. Let's move her over to the cavity room now!" Tara blurts out, as she motions to both of them to help her.

They place the lifeless body on an old two man carrying stretcher made from wood and thick canvas cloth and carry her down to another door in the basement at the very end of the hall. The door opens and they carry the body down a flight of stairs, twelve steps down. There is very low lighting, just enough to illuminate the dark musty area. The floor is nothing but dry dirt. You can see two pre-made holes in the dirt over in the far corner of this room and three spade shovels lean against the old dirt ridden brick wall next to the two holes. The two premade holes are four feet long, two feet wide and four feet deep. They don't set the stretcher down on the dirt floor. They just walk up next to the hole and tilt the stretcher over to the side and let the girl's lifeless mangled body flop into the small hole. Dust flies up into the air as her flesh hits the bottom of the shallow grave that will forever be her resting place. All three women pick up shovels and start throwing dirt down onto the girl's body, dust bellowing up around them. Christa starts to laugh uncontrollably and says, "I feel like I'm planting a god damn garden! I should throw down some weed seeds and call it day!" Tara and Mitch just look up at her and shake their heads slightly; Tara does get a slight smile on her face but puts her head down so the other two women can't see it. After about thirty minutes of throwing dirt in the hole, it is covered. They place the shovels back along the wall and go back up stairs to the main basement area and put everything back in its place. They turn off all the lights and go back to the main portion of the house and leave the chamber they have made. All three women get cleaned up and ready for bed as if it's just another normal day, like everyone else in the world around them. Off to shower and get some much needed rest after their fun filled evening.

Chapter 7

The smell of coffee fills the air in the beautifully kept farmhouse where the three girls all live. Tara has made a strong pot of coffee and is sitting down to watch some morning news to try and catch some weather so she can plan her day. She stares blankly at the TV as a photo of the girl they just killed is on the screen staring back at her, she hears a women's tearful voice talking to her through the TV. "Please, this is my daughter Caroline, if anyone has seen her please call the police. She's only sixteen and innocent, loving, caring, please don't hurt my baby. If you have her, let her go, I just want her back." Then they cut back to the newscaster on location with the mother of the girl they just murdered last night. "Well this is just a tragic story of another girl that has gone missing in the last few months. Hopefully someone has some information about this young girl so she can be returned back to her family. John, back to you." states the newscaster. Tara looks at the TV and says under her breath, "Innocent my ass, no sixteen year old girl is innocent anymore." Tara thinks about what a waste of time it was for that mother to have raised that young girl and now she's dead. Thinking about how people just waste their time, theirs lives raising their young and not truly living themselves. How if she was a good mother she would have protected her young from the evils of the world and not let her walk alone at night in the middle of nowhere. Tara gets a halfcocked smile on her face and just thinks, it serves that mother right for not protecting her young from harm. Even wild animals fight till the death to protect their young. "Wow, humans are so stupid, what a waste." Tara whispers to herself. Tara thinks back about her childhood but can't seem to remember it, anything about it. She doesn't know why she can't even think of one memory, but after a while she just shrugs it off and goes back to enjoying her morning.

Mitch walks into the kitchen and grabs a cup of coffee. "Good morning Mitch!" Tara says. "Good morning Tara, thanks for being understanding about last night. I'm sure you're not too happy with me about it. I just get so damn excited and an intense feeling just over takes me, sorry." Mitch tells Tara. Tara responds, "I know what you mean, that's why we get along so well, all of us. We all have the same intensity inside when we slowly torture and kill stupid humans, sexy humans. I would never waste my time on slowly killing a man though; I would just shoot him in the head and call it a day. I just get such a rush of taking my time with a pretty woman, caressing her body as I cut deep into her flesh. Always looking deep into her eyes and never forgetting that she indeed is a person with a life, a family. Just knowing that someone cares for her out there somewhere charges me up, we are not just taking one life, but the lives of everyone she loves and that loves her. It's like a ten for one sale." Mitch looks at her and lets out a laugh and a big smile then reaches out and places her hand on Tara's hand. "It's so funny how we are so much alike!" Mitch says. Tara replies, "I'm so glad we can just talk and be open with each other like this, I think if we didn't we would just crack and be miserable like the rest of the world. God knows I love Christa but I'm glad we are talking one on one about this without her here. I truly don't think anything bothers her, she just smokes her weed, laughs and loves life. I don't think she could be serious to really talk about it with us." Tara interrupts her own thought to say, "Oh I saw the mother of that girl we killed last night on the news this morning begging someone to bring her daughter back to her. What a fucking joke. It just makes me want to go get another one fast, let the world know, she doesn't matter, no one really matters in this vast world of shit. Even the other ones, the news doesn't even mention them anymore. No one cares; the only people who do care are their loved ones. Oh I saw another one of our dead little girl's parents at the store a couple weeks ago, looking so so sad. I had to get out of there fast, I just started busting out laughing when I saw their stupid faces." Mitch responds, "Well, just be careful about being to free with your emotions out there. We don't want people thinking we are heartless or anything." The girls then set off to shower and get ready for their day.

Chapter 8

Mitch sets out for the drive into Portland to her office. She examines her thoughts but can't come up with an answer as to why she can't be more calm and patient when she starts to open up a woman's body to touch their hearts. She thinks maybe because she's so tough and jaded to the world around her. Maybe growing up without a lot of love or any people that were close to her. Only people who said they loved her but lied behind her back and left her lonely and longing for more. Relationships that had no passion for anything just booze, sex and pain.

Mitch arrives at her office, a neat and clean office area that has nothing out of place, just like their house. She sets in for a day of paper work and calls to her officers around the world with what and when they need to deliver food, guns and other goods to the troops.

Mitch looks out her door to her office and sees one of the female clerks coming toward her and then the clerk walks into Mitch's office and sits down without being asked, just sits down and makes herself at home. The woman just stares at Mitch with a halfcocked smile. Mitch asks her, “Can I help you with something?” The woman responds with a slow and sexy tone. “Yes you can Mitch. I think we need to go for lunch today, I’ll pick the place, and you just meet me there. The answer of no is not an option by the way.” Before Mitch can even respond to her, the woman then slides a piece of paper across the desk to Mitch and then she walks out of Mitch’s office, she walks with an intentional strut to tease her. Mitch watches her walk away. A tall, slender, blonde haired woman with a long slit in the back of her black short skirt, black leggings and six-inch heels. Mitch looks back down to the piece of paper and it has the address of a hotel across town on it with a room number and time on it. A bright red kiss is on the paper made from the woman’s lipstick she was wearing. Mitch thinks about Tara for a moment and what a good talk they had, but she doesn't think on it too long. She then picks up the phone and lets her boss know she has to run errands the rest of the day and won't be back to the office. She hangs up the phone, and just can't help but think this is a weird turn of events for a Monday morning at a normally boring office.

Mitch jumps in her car and drives to the hotel, all the while she is thinking of the woman that passed her the note. She's not sure of her name, Kim maybe? Jane? She has seen her in the office for years and had thought of her before in a way that is almost evil. Never speaking to her but only seeing her pass by her office time and time again. Mitch wonders if this is a good idea, after all, they work together, and will see each other every day. Mitch is like any other human, an animal raging with lust inside of her. She knows she has to keep this lust in check, because her lusting can turn into a sick and twisted event of torture, hate driven passion that can explode out of control. No time to keep pondering it, Mitch arrives at the hotel, she looks around the parking lot, pans to the cross streets and doesn't see anything out of place. Just a moderate hotel, where the doors are all on the outside of it, nothing fancy but not too run down either. She has no idea what to expect, is this a setup of some kind or just an afternoon filled with hot passionate sex with a stranger from her office.

Mitch knocks on the door and the woman slowly opens the door to the hotel room. The woman is not in her work attire anymore, she's wearing a thin short black silk robe closed loosely. Six inch red heels with faux diamonds around the back of them, black stockings with a garter belt can barely be seen showing through just below the robe. She shows Mitch in, and closes the door behind her, five candles are lit, and no other light enters the room. She hands Mitch a glass of champagne in a crystal flute glass with soft music playing in the background. Mitch pulls out a flask with scotch in it and takes a few sips. Mitch asks the woman, “By the way, what’s your name? I’ve seen you around work but have no idea what your name is.” The woman doesn’t answer, she just walks up to Mitch and looks her in her eyes, slowly taking her hands around Mitch feeling her tight athletic tummy then around to her sides and up to her breasts, then takes one hand to the back of Mitch’s hair and runs her fingers through it, she then pulls her in close and goes in softly for a long passionate wet tongue filled kiss. Mitch drops her flask and returns the wet kiss and opens up the woman's silk robe caressing her breasts and lightly pinching her nipples. Mitch then pulls back from the kiss just to take a long look at the woman's sexy body, then placing her hand gently around the woman's neck from the front and just squeezes down a little bit, just enough to make her lose her breath for a few seconds. Mitch walks her backwards toward the bed and lays her down and goes back in for a high school point of no return kiss. Mitch works down her body with her hand, slipping it into the woman's black panties that are now wet from excitement and places her other hand over her heart to feel it beating out of her chest with anticipation. Mitch takes the woman's panties off, ripping them from her body. Mitch then flips the woman over and starts fucking her with her fingers from behind, so Mitch doesn't have to make eye contact with her. The woman is moaning out in pure excitement and pleasure clawing at the sheets on the bed. Mitch takes the woman's hand and puts it in her pants on her hot wet pussy and masturbates with the woman's hand while continuing to fuck the woman from behind. Mitch's mind starts to race and is taken down a dark tunnel of blood soaked bodies screaming out in pain. Her thoughts take her to all the woman she has tortured and spoke softly yet sweetly to while cutting them apart. Mitch cums quickly and almost violently, but yet holding back any loud screams or moans, just soft slight moaning, heavy intense breathing and the tightening of her whole body in pleasure at the intense climax of their fucking. The woman starts to climax uncontrollably as she hears

Mitch softly moan in climax in her ear, she can feel how tense Mitch is as she cums over her hand and feels her swollen wet clit on her fingers. The woman starts to laugh out loud and explode in excitement as she feels so good, and hasn't ever felt an orgasm so intense and fast. Mitch falls to the bed next to her on the bed as they try and catch their breath after such an intense erotic but fast experience. The woman runs her fingers through Mitch's hair and leans in and starts kissing Mitch softly teasing her with her tongue on her lips and tongue. Mitch starts down the woman's glistening body with small kisses working her way down past her stomach to her inner thighs as one hand is pinching one of her nipples and the other hand is slowly rubbing her inner thigh area next to her pussy, then kissing her way to her still very swollen wet clit.

Mitch slowly starts lightly licking and sucking on her swollen clit driving the woman crazy. Mitch takes her hand from the woman's nipple and moves it up to her neck and firmly places her hand around the woman's thin soft neck and squeezes as she continues to lick and suck on her clit. The woman doesn't fight Mitch at all. Mitch's grasp becomes more tightly gripped around the woman's throat, her face starts to turn red, veins popping out slightly around her head and neck area, her eyes watering and turning slightly pink to red as Mitch squeezes harder. The woman feels light headed but then starts to cum hard, trying to breath as she cums, her body starts to flair a bit as Mitch sucks her clit while she cums, her clit is swollen in Mitch's mouth and she can taste every bit of her sweet delicious pussy in her mouth. Mitch slowly releases her grip from around her throat as she is still having a few small multiple orgasms after the huge indescribable climax she has ever had in her plentiful sex life. The woman just lies there slightly shaking from the last few flicks of Mitch's tongue and oxygen starts coming back into the woman's body and to her brain. As the oxygen starts to come back, the woman just starts to laugh as tears roll down her face, she truly has never felt so good. Mitch moves up on the bed lying next to the woman, and starts to kiss her neck and then kisses her lips a few times, Mitch pulls away and gets up from the bed and walks over to her flask, quickly picks it up and takes a drink. Mitch knows she has to get out of there before she can't stop herself, the woman is so gorgeous and is just what Mitch likes for her torture sessions. "Thanks for the fuck" Mitch says, as she washes her hands, cleans up, and checks herself in the mirror. "By the way, what's your name?" Mitch asks. "Diana, my name is Diana. That's it? You're just going to leave now? Don't you want to keep this going all night?" Replies Diana. Mitch just looks at her, winks, blows her a kiss and walks out of the hotel room, leaving Diana hot and wanting more lying there naked on the bed. Diana can't believe she just walked out on her, just leaving her lying there naked and worked up in the mist of the sheets strewn about on the bed. Diana is left with a stunned look of disbelief on her face and a longing for more throughout every inch of her body.

Mitch gets into her vehicle and makes the drive home and she thinks about Diana and Tara. She knows she shouldn't have had sex with

Diana, but like any animal, how can a human resist hot, exciting, no strings attached sex with a sexy piece of flesh like Diana. Mitch knows by telling Tara, it could ruin everything, a possible new romantic relationship between them and the trust that they have in their friendship of torture and secrets that binds them together. Mitch just turns on the radio for the rest of her drive home staring blankly at the road with a halfcocked smile on her face.

Chapter 9

Tara is sitting at the kitchen table thumbing through a magazine and sipping on a tall glass of iced tea. The television is on but turned down low, you can just barely make out the noise coming from it. Christa walks into the kitchen and goes into the fridge for a bottle of water. She walks over to the table and runs her fingers through Tara's hair on her way to the chair at the other end of the kitchen table. "What the hell?" Tara yelled. Christa looks blankly at Tara and places her tongue between two fingers in front of her mouth and vigorously moves her tongue up and down for a few seconds. Tara is looking at her when she does it. "That's real mature." Tara states without emotion. She goes back to looking at her magazine, not reading it, just looking through it at the pictures.

Christa takes out a joint from behind her ear and lights up, taking a hard long puff from it. As she exhales the smoke from her lungs and out between her lips, the sounds of gravel under tires can be heard through the window. "Someone is pulling up." Christa said. Tara gets up and looks out the kitchen window, as she looks out she can see it's Mitch pulling up into the drive way. "She's home early." Tara mutters under her breath with a raised eyebrow. Tara watches Mitch get out of her car and slowly walk up to the house, Mitch has sunglasses on and her normal workbag with her but something looks different about her expression. Mitch being home so early perplexes Tara. Mitch never comes home early. If anything she is always running behind due to her work. Tara just stays in the kitchen and sits back down at the table and tries not to give it another thought as Mitch walks in the front door and then heads right up to her room without as much as a hello or a, I'm home to either of them. Tara sits there for a few minutes with her arms crossed at the table but can't take the not knowing what's going on with Mitch. Tara truly cares for her and wants Mitch to know she is there for her, anytime for any reason. Tara walks to the stairs then pauses; she wonders if maybe something happened, maybe someone found out about what they are doing at the farmhouse. Her mind fills with thoughts of the police heading up the driveway with lights and sirens blaring, the police busting down the door with guns blazing. Throwing them to the ground and cuffing them like animals, finding the rooms in the basement. Being seen all over the news for everyone to condemn them for what they have done. "They'll never understand the purpose." Tara says quietly but loud enough to be heard. As Tara still stands at the base of the stairs with one hand on the polished wooden banister, Mitch walks down the stairs and grabs her hand. "What did you just say Tara?" Mitch asks. Tara feels Mitch's touch and it slowly brings her out of her thoughts and back into reality. Tara says loudly, “What?” Mitch responds, “Where were you just now, you sure where lost in something Tara.” Tara just laughs it off with a half crazy half jumpy smile on her face.

Mitch sits down at the kitchen table. Tara comes over and leans against the counter where the sink is. “We need to make a small trip, maybe head south down into California. I’m thinking we can take two girls instead of just one to throw off what the F.B.I. knows about the case.” Mitch tells the other ladies. The other two ladies are slightly shaking their heads yes as to acknowledge what was just said. “I agree Mitch and we will go this weekend. Christa can stay here.” Tara says. The ladies all agree and will head out this weekend, which are a couple short days away. The look of excitement comes over all of their faces at the thought of getting a two for one. They all just go about the rest of the day as evening is setting in on the farmhouse.

Mitch goes downstairs to the basement and into the hidden rooms that lie beyond the walls. Mitch walks through all the rooms to do a check of everything. She checks the chains attached to a metal pole that is sunk down into the cement. These are holding rooms where girls are chained by their wrists until they are ready for them once they get each girl back to the house. The rooms are small with a toilet; no shower just a hose on the wall with a drain in the cement floor. There is a thin mat with no blanket in there as well in case it may be days until they have their fun with them. There are only two of these holding rooms. On the door to the rooms there is a peek hole looking in, so they can see what their captives are doing before the open they door. Safety first. They know once you take someone and their lives are threatened, humans are like any wild animal that wants to live, they can be very dangerous to handle without any precautions. Everything looks to be in order throughout all the rooms.

Mitch flips on the light in the one room with the girl in it and looks through the peek hole, the girl puts up one of her hands to block the light from her eyes. Mitch opens the door and asks her if she is ok and if she needs anything. The girl just looks at her, and for the first time can see Mitch's face in the light. The woman is not sure which one this is, but thinks it is the one who raped her after being tortured. Fear over comes her but she stuffs it back down inside herself and just answers Mitch so she doesn't make her mad. "No, I'm not ok, I want to leave, please let me go, I swear I won't say anything, just please let me go." the girl pleads to Mitch in a quite meek voice. Mitch just smiles at her and gets closer to her. "I'm going to check your hand." Mitch unwraps the girl's left hand and takes a look, just a little red but not bad. Mitch goes and gets new bandages and some betadine and cleans it up again and re-wraps her hand where her thumb is missing. "See, I'm not a monster." Mitch says. Mitch then leans in and gives her a small kiss on her cheek. As Mitch walks out and starts to close the door, the girl says thank you to Mitch. Mitch just smiles and shuts the lights out and locks the door. The girl is hoping that maybe, just maybe she can win her over and be let go, she knows it's probably not going to happen but she has to try something. The woman just breaks down sobbing in the dark as she hears the sound of the loud metal door being locked.

Mitch then goes to the room covered in plastic with the embalming table in it. She laid down on the embalming table and thinks back about her meeting in the hotel room earlier in the day. Between thinking about that and being in the room where they torture women, she can't help herself. She unbuttons and unzips her jeans and slides her hand down her pants and places her middle finger on her clit and starts to massage it slowly and gently as she lies on the cold metal table. Her thoughts go to the woman from her office being secured down to the table wearing just a black bra, black silk panties with garter belts hooked to black panty hose. In

Mitch's mind she images the woman being so intensely aroused with no fear and this just being a room that Mitch has to keep things kinky and exciting for sex play. Mitch changes gears in her mind; she imagined she pulls out a five-inch bladed knife and runs it sideways down her body so it wouldn't cut her, running it from her neck to down to her pussy. The woman's eyes begin to fill with fear and starts telling Mitch she's not into that kind of sex, Mitch cuts off her panties and shoves them into her mouth to shut her up. Mitch starts rubbing her clit faster and harder while slipping her finger inside herself every now and again as she thinks of the woman being in her torture chamber. Mitch's thoughts then go to the knife cutting into the woman's flesh just below her left breast. Blood starts to ooze out and run down the woman's side onto the cold metal table. Mitch gets overly excited and cums intensely, she can't keep quiet, she moans loudly and her body is shaking from cumming so hard. As Mitch lay on the table catching her breath she comes back into reality, her knees are weak and her body feels so relaxed. She awkwardly slides off from the table and washes her hands in the sink, then fixes her hair a bit while checking her face in a mirror just outside the room. She tries to collect herself before going back upstairs. The ladies do a lot of things together and share things most people could never even fathom, but ladies should still keep their masturbation habits to themselves, or at least be a lady about it.

Chapter 10

A couple of days go by. Mitch and Tara get a small bag together for their short trip just in case they need to stay a night in a hotel. They both say goodbye to Christa and are off down the road to find not just one but two victims. They would never refer to women they take as victims themselves however. In the car together they don't really say too much to each other, Mitch just sips coffee as she drives. Tara is just staring out the window while the radio plays; just talk radio with news of the day is on this early in the morning unless you want to listen to gospel or the oldies. There is still some slight tension between them, nothing bad, just knowing they are going to try and make a relationship between them and the awkward nervous silence when you like someone. It's almost like two people who just met, with shyness and both are just unsure about how to really proceed without messing up their friendship. Tara turns and looks at Mitch, she places her hand on Mitch's leg as she drives. "What are you looking for this time? Anything in particular or just anything that's hot, sexy and easy to grab up?" Tara asks. "I think we should get one sexy blonde and one sexy brunette chick, and as far as easy, if it were easy everyone would be doing it. Safe, that's all I care about, that we are safe. Watch out for cameras, which are everywhere now." Mitch responded.

"That sounds good to me, one blonde and one sexy ass brunette! Let's stop somewhere and get a bite to eat, I need to get out and stretch my legs too, we have been on the road a while." Tara said.

They pull off the highway, after driving for a few hours, at the next exit with signs of life on it. They see a little pancake house slash truck stop so they go ahead and pull in there. A cool little place as far as truck stops go. It has a restaurant, gas station and souvenir shop with the usual magnets, ashtrays and the like lining the inside. They walk through and see all different types of people, families traveling together, a few businessmen, and of course truck drivers. Some dirty and fat, looking as if they never stop to shower or sleep and others that are thin, clean and well kept. They are seated at a booth and they can see the layout of the restaurant pretty well from where they sit. The ladies order breakfast, nothing fancy, just some pancakes and eggs. Mitch scans around checking everyone out; she spots a nice looking female with short brown hair, fare skin and green eyes. The woman is wearing an old green army jacket, blue jeans with a few worn areas in them and brown hiking boots. She is sitting alone at a smaller booth reading something on a tablet while sipping coffee. Mitch watches her as she and Tara eat their breakfast. Mitch doesn't say anything to Tara about it, she just keeps watching her to make sure she is truly alone. They finish up and pay the check with cash and head out for the car.

Once they get into the car Mitch tells Tara about the young woman in the restaurant with them. The parking lot is full of cars traveling here and there and people coming and going not paying attention to anything but themselves, so they wait in the car watching the door for the girl to come out. “If she comes out and heads for the highway we will follow her on the road, if she goes down the road without getting on the highway, we will just keep moving on looking for someone else. Just in case she is local around here and people might be watching.” Mitch tells Tara while waiting for her to come out of the restaurant. “Ok, that sounds good to me too.” Tara responded.

The young woman comes out of the truck stop restaurant and heads for a small pickup truck and gets in, she starts heading out and goes onto the highway, in the same direction that Mitch and Tara where headed in before they had stopped for a bite to eat. They wait a minute or so and then head for the highway behind her; they keep a nice pace behind her, not getting too close but just keeping with her down the road. An hour and forty minutes have gone by and finally the young woman exits off the highway. They slow their speed to see where she is headed and to keep distance between them so it doesn't seem like they are following her. The woman stops at a gas station to fill up. The gas station is pretty full of people coming and going, no one is really paying attention to anything, just trying to get what they need and get on with their day.

Mitch and Tara pull up at the small pump but on the opposite side, Tara gets out of the car and comes around to the driver's side of the car and opens up the door to the back seat and gets in. Mitch gets out of the car and is acting like she is going to be pumping gas. She has a towel in one hand. Mitch looks around and again no one is even paying attention to anything, Mitch also doesn't see any cameras outside. As soon as the woman hangs up the handle from pumping her gas, Mitch asks her if she has any jumper cables. The woman didn't really hear Mitch so she walked over to her on the other side of the pump. "I'm sorry, did you ask me for jumper cables?" the woman asked. Right then Mitch grabbed her arm with one hand and shoved the towel into the woman's mouth with the other hand so she couldn't scream out. Mitch quickly shoved her into the back seat with Tara. Tara held her down and placed chloroform over her nose, keeping her held there by grasping the woman's arms together with her legs around her so the woman couldn't move. Mitch calmly gets into the car and drives away, as she drives away she checks her rearview mirror and no one is even looking. The whole act only took seconds to get the woman into the car and drive away.

The sounds of duct tape coming off the roll can be heard from the back seat, Tara is taping the woman's wrists and ankles together and places a small piece over the towel in her mouth so when she wakes up she can't scream out or make too much noise. "Everything ok back there?" Mitch asks Tara. "Yes, pull over so I can get into the front with you. I have pretty much hog-tied her, so we are good to go." Mitch pulls over and Tara gets out of the back seat, as she gets out she leans back in and rolls the woman toward the floor of the car and then places a blanket over the girl so no one can see anyone in the backseat as they drive down the road. “Well that went pretty damn smooth I must say. Right under the noses of all those people. Isn’t it funny how people are so self-involved now that they don’t even care what is happening around them?” Tara says to Mitch. Mitch just smiles and winks at Tara and keeps driving down the road. “Did you check her pockets for any cell phones or anything? ‘ Mitch asks Tara. “Yes, nothing in her pockets of her pants or jacket, I double checked.” Tara responded. “Good, we don’t need anyone tracking that.” Mitch said.

Chapter 11

Hours and hours have passed, back at the gas station the attendant inside finally notices that a small pickup truck has been at the same pump and hasn't moved. Pump number nine. The attendant calls over the manager and tells him about the small truck. The manager goes outside and walks slowly over to the truck, finding the window down, purse open, just sitting on the seat and the keys are in the ignition but nothing looks out of sorts. The manager goes back in and checks the restrooms and looks around the station but doesn't find anyone that the truck belongs to. The manager calls out the police to come and check it out.

The local police arrive on scene and look around, they look in her purse for identification, her driver's license says Becky Dovall, age 22, and they also find a collage ID as well. They check her tablet to see what Becky had been doing or looking at earlier that day in hopes it could help them find out how this young woman just disappeared into thin air. The local police make a call to the F.B.I. to see if this is in anyway related to the other missing girls from the surrounding states as of late. Once the F.B.I. gets the call they have a couple of agents on scene right away. They get her photo and information out over the internet to the surrounding states and their police agencies within moments of them getting to the gas station and checking things out.

Mitch's phone goes off, it's an alert she has from the state police. She has the alerts set up for whenever they have something really big going on or when a girl is reported missing through the system. Since Mitch works at the private security agency that works with the U.S. government she has access to these alerts and reports as they come out. Mitch checked her phone and sees it is for the woman in the back seat of their car. "Well it took them long enough, it's only been hours and hours." Mitch says to

Tara. Mitch tells Tara about the alert that has gone out, and that her name is Becky.

Back at the gas station the FBI are going through the car and running back receipts for everyone that paid with a credit or debit card that day. They have nothing to go on, no leads of any kind, even her tablet doesn't even help, she was reading a book on it, nothing more. They did contact her family, they called a couple of agents that are closer to where her parents live to go over and first question her family and friends there. They told them the news about her being missing and that they found her pickup truck and her belongings still in it at the gas station. The family had no information. They didn't even know why she would be traveling. They thought she was at school. They had just talked to her two days earlier on the phone and Becky didn't mention anything about that or anything else, just that she was doing well in school and she missed them. The agents went through her room but she has been away at school for months. The father found some phone numbers for a few of Becky's friends and gave them to the FBI agents. The mother just breaks down into tears and doesn't know how to even process this information at all. How could she just be gone, why would this happen, did she walk away or did someone take her? The father tries to console the mother but she just starts hitting him and wants him off of her, she pushes his comforting arms away. The agents tell them that they will be in touch if they hear anything or have more questions. The agents leave and the parents are just left with a huge emptiness, no answers, no reasons, and no hope.

Chapter 12

Back on the road, night has now fallen and Mitch tells Tara it's time to stop somewhere for the night since they have been driving for hours. Moans and soft sounds of crying are coming from the backseat. They see a light off in the distance as they get closer and see it's for a small motel, not a chain but a mom and pop type single level motel. They get off the highway and pull up to the small rundown motel; only one car is in the lot. The motel needs paint and not all the lights are working by the doors to the rooms or in the parking lot. The motel is setup in a U shape with the office on the end, all rooms facing each other and into the parking lot.

They pull up in front of the motel office. Mitch stays in the car with the motor running and the windows up with the radio on just in case someone comes by. Tara goes in to get the room and scans the outside and the inside of the office as she walks in. Tara doesn't see anyone so she calls out, 'Hello? Is there anyone here?" A young lady comes out from the back, "Hi there, how can I help you this evening?" The young clerk asked with a big happy smile on her face. Tara informs her that they just need a room for the night and Tara laid down her ID card as she pulls out some cash from her pocket to pay for the room. The clerk checks them in and hands Tara a key to a room in the middle of motel, the clerk tells Chrissy to have a good night and to let her know if there is anything they need for their stay. Tara turns around and says thanks and walks out, Tara's ID card is a fake ID card she had made up so she never has to use her real name on runs.

Tara walks to the room and Mitch pulls the car over to the room, which is six rooms down from the motel office. Tara and Mitch go into the room, turn the lights on and look around first, they turn the television on for noise, and the only other noise is the cars going by on the highway. They go out to the car to get the young lady from the backseat; they look around, don't see anyone, so they open the back passenger door, Mitch grabs her under her arms and pulls her out. Her legs flop out onto the parking lot, she moans but cannot scream out, she chokes a little on the gag in her mouth. Tara grabs her legs around the ankles and they quickly move her into the room and close the door, the girl doesn't struggle much. She is still tied up and gagged. They face her toward the wall so the young lady can't see what they are doing. Tara gets out her MP3 player and puts the ear buds in the ladies ears and turns it on so she can't hear anything they do or say or what's going on around her. Tara goes outside the motel room and shuts the door and lights up a cigarette and just looks and listens to make sure no one is out and about. Tara only hears a few cars passing by from the highway as she takes a slow drag from the cigarette. She doesn't smoke but does this so it just doesn't seem odd that she is just standing outside, looking around, watching. She doesn't inhale the smoke, just puffs and blows the smoke back out. Tara goes back into the room and lets Mitch know nothing is going on outside, no movement, no people.

With the music playing loudly in her ears the young woman can only see slight shadows on the wall she is facing, but it's barely a shadow as the lights are on in the room. She can also feel the slight vibrations as they walk around close to her. All her senses are heightened, but fear is overcoming her whole body and mind, not knowing who these people are or what is even happening, all the young woman knows is she is in a fucked up situation. She's trying to think, did she do anything to piss someone off? Did she wrong someone without being aware of it? Are there more people coming to meet them here? Sweat is beading up on her upper lip and forehead, tears start to roll down her cheek to the old dirty smelly motel carpet, but she tries to fight back the tears so they won't see her crying, she doesn't want to give them any kind of power. She tells herself to be strong but her lips keep quivering around the gag in her mouth. She just keeps flashing to movies she has seen, how people are taken, raped, tortured or sold as sex slaves and forced to have sex with nasty men, gang raped or worse, sex with animals. Thoughts just racing and racing through her mind when out of nowhere the ear buds are ripped from her ears. She can feel a breath on her neck and ear, then a soft whisper comes. Mitch whispers softly and slowly to her, "Don't scream out, don't try to get away from us and you'll get through this just fine. We don't want to hurt you but we will if we need too. Let's get through this together, and then you can go home again. We just want the money, ok?" Then the ear buds go back in the girl's ears and the music blares, she doesn't understand what they are even talking about, what money? Her family doesn't have any money, are they selling her she wonders. She feels the rag come out of her mouth and she feels something small and round being shoved into her mouth, it tastes nasty. Then she is grabbed and forced to sit up, she can't hear or see anything, then water is brought up to her mouth and she drinks down some of the water and swallows some pills. Mitch has just given her sleeping pills so she will just fall asleep for a while. They drag the lady over to the bed and tie her arms around one of the bed legs so they can keep her in one spot. She can feel the sharp edges from the bed leg and her arms are being pulled behind her hurting her back, she feels like she is in certain hell. She dare not make a sound or try and move for fear of what they will do to her, she tries to lie very still no matter how bad the pain and rotting smell is. They both lie down and try and get some sleep for the drive back and hopefully to get another girl on the way back, but they need much needed sleep.

Chapter 13

The sun is just peeking out from beyond the earth, filling the sky, another beautiful day. Christa wakes early back at the house, fixes her a nice strong cup of coffee and watches the sun rise through the trees and she wonders how Mitch and Tara are doing and hoping they are ok. Christa wonders why they never ask her to go with them, as she stares out the window, as she ponders about this, it hits her! "I'll show them I can get a girl too!" she says out loud to herself. Christa gets herself together for the day, showered and dressed. She goes out to the pickup truck and looks through it for anything she might need. She goes back into the house, gets a small 22 caliber pistol, duct tape and a pillowcase. "That's all I should need to get a girl, I'll show them." Christa says.

She gets into the pick-up truck and starts out to the road, it's still morning and a bright beautiful day out. She keeps driving around back roads and on and off the highway for about an hour or so, all the sudden she sees a lady walking down the side of the highway, Christa pulls over just in front of her and waits for the lady to get closer. “Hi, do you need some help? Can I call someone for you?” Christa asks the lady. “I just know I would want someone to stop and help me if I was walking down the highway.” The lady responds. “Well normally I wouldn’t take help from a stranger but you look like a sweet little thing. If I could just get a ride to the closest gas station that would be great! I ran out of gas. I can’t believe it.” Christa tells the lady to jump in the passenger side and they take off down the road. “Thanks for helping me out, I feel like I have been walking forever out there.” Christa replies, “No problem, there’s not a lot out here for sure, we are kind of in the middle of nowhere.” Then Christa laughs. Christa then pulls out the gun and points it at her. The lady’s eyes instantly open wide and her mouth drops open a bit. She can’t believe she is now looking down the barrel of a gun, the lady just can't scream out or move, she is frozen in fear. All the sudden, Christa takes the gun and hits the lady in the head hard, she does this two times. The lady is shaken and now bleeding out of her head. Christa pulls over in a hurry and gets out the duct tape and wraps it around her mouth going all the way around her head and then grabs her wrists and duct tapes them as well. Christa then shoves the lady down to the floorboards and kicks her in the head again. "Don't you move or I will blow your fucking head off bitch!" Christa tells the lady as she gets back on the highway and heads for home. Christa is on cloud nine, all the adrenaline pumping through her body, she feels better than taking any kind of drug, her hands are shaking and she just can't get the big smile from ear to ear off her face. She takes in some big breaths to calm her down as she drives. The drive back to the house takes just under an hour, and she keeps looking around and over her shoulder on her way back.

Christa pulls into the long winding driveway, she lets out a big excited sigh. Glad she's back safe and sound to the house. She gets out and walks over to the passenger side of the truck and opens the door, the lady's eyes are wide open and tears are coming down her face, she is trying to shake her head no. Christa pulls out the gun and shows it to the lady and says, "We can do this the hard way, or we can do it my way bitch, got it?" Christa then pulls her out of the truck and stands her up on her own two feet and walks the lady into the house. The lady turns fast and tries to run and Christa quickly fires a shot into her left leg. The lady falls onto the porch in pain, screaming, but her mouth is still duct taped over. Christa grabs her and pulls her into the house, gets her to the stairs and just shoves the lady down into the darkness. "We could have done it my way, now we are doing it the fucking hard way!" Christa yells down the stairs to her. Now Christa is mad and cussing under her breath, she goes down stairs and gets the lady into the hidden area, and chains her in one of the small rooms that only has a toilet and tile on the floor. After the lady is secured and chained, Christa takes her duct tape gag off and then wraps the ladies leg up to keep the bleeding down. "Now I have to go clean up your mess you stupid bitch!" Christa yells, then slams the door and goes back up to clean up the blood from the front porch and that has been dragged through the house.

Christa's anger starts to wear off as she is cleaning up the blood from the floor; she just keeps thinking how happy Mitch and Tara will be with her, as long as she can get this blood up. After cleaning the floor, porch and the stairwell she double checks all areas, bucket and rags, to make sure no blood can be seen anywhere. "There, you would never know anything ever happened here."

Christa goes down to the hidden area in the basement. Christa slowly walks down the short hallway and puts her ear up to the door where the lady is chained up. Christa doesn't hear anything in the room. She opens the door and flips on the light, the lady covers her eyes from the light and tries to see who is coming into the room. Her eyes start to adjust to the light in room and she sees Christa just standing there in the doorway. "What are you going to do with me?" the lady asks. Christa replies, "Well right now I'm going to clean you up and take a look at you, see what you're all about. You look ok, thin, I bet your pretty when you're all cleaned up. I want you to take these pills, they are sleeping pills, and they will help us both. I'm going to get you cleaned up and I don't need you getting crazy so these will help relax you. You already know I will hurt you and I don't want to do that, well not right now anyway. So just take these pills and I'll come back in a little while ok?" The lady knows she is in a really bad spot and doesn't want to make her mad again, she shakes her head yes and agrees to take the pills. As she takes the pills, her hands are trembling and she starts to cry slightly. Christa checks her mouth to make sure she took the pills and then flips out the light again and shuts and locks the door behind her.

Christa goes upstairs and looks at the clock. It is now late afternoon early evening. She wonders if Mitch and Tara will be back tonight, she's so excited she doesn't know what to do, she needs to keep busy to take her mind off of it. She starts cleaning up the house a bit, light dusting and mops the floors like it's just another day in the country as she hums to the radio as she cleans. She goes back down to the hidden area to check on her prize she has gotten and to see if the pills have taken affect so she can get the lady cleaned up. Christa grabs soap, a hose and some makeup before going into the room where the lady is, and she opens the door and finds her half in half out of sleep. "Well hello there, I'm going to get you cleaned up." Christa tells her. She hooks up the hose and makes sure the water temperature isn't too cold or too hot. She strips her naked, cutting and ripping her clothes off around the chains and throwing them off to the side, as she throws the clothes she hears something hit and bounce off the tile. It's a small cell phone, Christa's face goes blank and she walks over and takes the battery out of the phone. "Whew, that could have been bad." She then throws the cell phone onto the pile of clothes and hoses the lady down, soaping her up and rinsing her off. The lady tries to fight back a little but can't because she is too groggy from the pills. Christa turns off the hose then dry's her off a bit and runs her fingers through her hair while looking at her face and body. "We need to get you looking nice for them, I'm going to put some makeup on you." Christa starts to put a little makeup on the lady's face, some base, little bit of eye shadow and lipstick, not the best makeup job as the woman tries to move and fight a bit. She looks like a washed out, fucked up, drugged out clown. "There we go, all pretty." Christa gives her a bottle of water and picks up the lady's clothes and cell phone to take out of the room, she takes them to the dirt area to be buried later. Christa double- checks the lock on the door and then checks in on the other girl, giving her some water and a bag of chips. She doesn't say anything to her and just closes the door, shuts the lights off and locks the door. She then goes back upstairs to wait for the ladies to return home.

Chapter 14

Mitch and Tara have already gotten around for the day and got the girl back in the car. They have put her in trunk, her hands and legs are hog-tied and she has a rag back in her mouth with a towel around her head so she can't see anything. She hears the car start and feels it start to move, straight, then turning as she is helpless and just flops around with every stop and turn of the car. All she can hear is the road going by mile after mile under her, the rattling of the car itself. As she listens to the road going by it almost puts her in a trance, thinking about her life, the fun with her friends as they would just talk and bullshit with each other, thinking about if she would ever see her family again and why the fuck this was happening to her. The trunk smells of old oil and rubber, she guesses from the spare tire she lies on. She just wishes she could see inside the trunk. See anything around her. As Mitch and Tara make their way back to the farmhouse, they still need to find another girl to take back with them. They do need to hurry, as they will need to return to work in another day.

“Look there.” Mitch says to Tara as she points to a sign to a hiking area off the road up ahead. “Let’s go check it out, see what kind of trails or what’s down there.” People do like to hike and run alone don’t they?” Tara said. They follow the road down to a small parking area with a trailhead. They park and go over to the trailhead, the sign says there are two different trails, a three mile trail and five mile trail. There are four cars in the parking area. They see a couple coming back down the trail. As they get closer Mitch yells out to them, “How are the trails?” The man answers back, “Short but good.”

“Rugged and narrow trails, you’ll love it!” “Thanks!” Mitch replies. They watch them get into their car and drive off down the road. “Well I don’t see why we can’t just hang out here for a bit and see if anyone comes down the trail alone or pulls up to park." As they sit there waiting, Mitch stares off into the beauty of the area around them, the trees and the rocks. "This is really pretty out here, nice and quite. I can see why people would come out here. We should really do some hiking soon." Mitch says to Tara. Tara just looks over smiles at her and touches her hand. "I'm so glad you're so sensitive, it's cute Mitch." Tara just can't stop smiling at her.

Just then a young woman comes down the trail heading to the parking lot area. Mitch goes into the car, leans in and grabs a syringe filled with a little bit of general anesthetic and cups it in her hand. She looks around as she approaches the young girl. "Hi there, do you have any jumper cables by chance?" Mitch asks her while walking toward her with a smile. "I do, you guys broke down huh? Let me get them for you and I'll move my car to help you guys out, I know how bad it sucks to be broken down somewhere." The girl walks to the back of her small SUV and opens the door while she is trying to catch her breath after coming off the trail. Mitch walks right up on her and sticks the needle in her neck, the woman's eyes pop open wide while her heart is racing she can't believe what's happening. The girl jumps back and tries to run and hop into her car, but everything seems like it's going in slow motion for her. But it's too late as the small amount of anesthesia is already taking effect on her small tired shaking frame of a body and she can't fight Mitch off. She feels Mitch's hands grab her, arms incasing her body so she can't move at all, almost like a Boa constrictor. Mitch has been trained in combat among other things so it's just useless for the woman to even try and escape. As the woman is going limp, everything fades to darkness as sound seems to be getting farther and farther away until there is nothing, the woman is now like a lifeless rag doll. Mitch drags her over to the car and puts her in the back seat. Mitch then goes back to the small SUV and shuts the back door, making sure not to touch it with her hand, then gives another look around to make sure no one else is around. Mitch slowly walks back to the car and gets in the driver's seat. Tara is in the back seat tying the young woman's hands together then tying her arms to the woman's legs. After Tara makes sure the girl is secured, she pats the woman down once again checking her for anything on her, phone, keys, or ID. She finds a phone, takes the battery out and throws it into the wooded area just off the parking lot, making sure to hold the phone with a small towel as to not leave any prints behind.

They back out and pull out onto the road and drive back to the highway slowly while watching in the rearview mirror. Back on the highway they are ready to get home and they have about a four-hour drive ahead of them to get back. “I bet she didn’t think her day would end up like that.” Tara says with a smile. “Sometimes I feel like it’s wrong to just take people and do whatever we want. If someone ever took you, I would hunt them down and kill them.” Mitch said to Tara. “ Well you can’t think like that, most people are bad inside and don’t care about anything anymore, just themselves, so it’s no loss to the world, people don’t have morals anymore. There are starving animals and homeless people all over, no one seems to care about them. Fuck them!" Tara replied. They just look at each other and bust out a big laugh and shake their heads as the drive down the highway back toward home. They can barely keep their breath and tears start to form in their eyes, as they just can't stop laughing until their stomach starts to hurt.

Chapter 15

Night falls on the farmhouse and Christa hears tires in the gravel, she runs to the window to see if it's the girls, sure enough they are pulling up out front. She runs to the door and flies through it outside to greet them with a big smile on her face. "I'm so glad you guys are back, I missed you so much!" Christa yells out to them as they barely come to a stop with the car. "So much has happened you guys!" Christa says with pure excitement and a huge smile on her face as she just stands there waiting for them to get out of the car.

Tara and Mitch get out of the car and both stretch out after the long drive home without a care in the world, or any worry of two women being in the car. Mitch opens the back door to check on the jogger, she is awake but out of it somewhat still. Mitch reaches in the back seat and grabs her by the rope behind the woman and pulls her out of the back seat, the woman is just dropped onto the dusty driveway like a heavy dirty bag of laundry. As the woman hits the driveway some dust flies up and she starts to choke and gag a little and making her throat even dryer then it already is from no water for hours. The woman can't see anything, she can only smell and hear what is going on around her. The unknown is getting to be almost unbearable for her, but there is nothing she can do about anything, a feeling most of us will never know to be this helpless, like a pig being taken to slaughter with no hope in sight. Christa jumps up and down clapping her hands lightly together as she sees the woman. "Hey she looks like a good one, did you guys get one or two?" Christa asks with a happy cheerleader enthusiasm.

Mitch walks over to the trunk and pops it open and Christa can't believe her eyes, another girl tied up, Christa is all too excited she slaps the woman in the trunk a few times on her ass while having an ear to ear grin on her face. The woman just moans a little as she can't speak through the towel gag, she is very awake and very aware of every sound and touch happening, though she cannot see anything going on around her. Mitch asks Christa for her help on getting the woman out of the trunk, Christa grabs her under her knees and Mitch grabs her behind her arms tied behind her back, they get her to the edge of the trunk and just drop her to the dirt. There is a small thud with dust flying up, she moans out through her gag as she hits the ground and can feel the dirt and gravel underneath her. The woman is trying to move around but can't move at all, just very small wiggles here and there, she relaxes her head onto the gravel and just waits for what is to come next, she just prays everything will be ok in this utter hell she has been thrown into.

"Okay, let's get these ladies inside, I'm tired and just want to relax after our trip for a little while." Mitch says. Mitch tells both women she is going to cut the rope from around their legs so they can walk on their own somewhat, but she is leaving the blindfolds on and gags in their mouths and arms tied up. Mitch takes out a big knife, with a seven-inch blade on it and cuts through the rope like butter. The girls help them up to their feet while hanging on to them so the two woman don't fall as they slowly walk them up the stairs on the porch and in through the front door of the farmhouse. As the girls walk in moving very slowly, almost shuffling their feet they are trying to hear anything to tell them where on earth they might be, or what kind of place it is. One woman can feel carpet that smells of fresh cleaners, the other woman is just too into her own darkness and fear to really notice anything around her. Mitch tells them to watch their step, as they are getting ready to walk down some stairs now, to take their time and be careful. The one woman can't believe she is hearing someone telling her to be careful, really? Be careful! Are you fucking kidding me! That's all she can think, by that time, they are at the bottom of the stairs now and still shuffling along with their feet slowly. "Ok, we have reached your final destination ladies!" Tara exclaims. They open the hidden door in the basement and walk them in and lock the door behind them. They can smell a musty mixed with bleach odor as they enter through the door and can hear the door being locked. Everything seems so intense, all their senses heightened. The jogger woman's heart is racing and she just feels sickened inside, to the point of passing out or throwing up with horrible thoughts running through her mind. She thinks of a few horrible things, rape or being killed but just can't wrap her head around what is really happening to her. Her body just trembles with unexplainable fear and panic. The college student is being calm and just trying to take in all the smells and sounds around her, she only hears women's voices and hasn't heard or felt a man touch her since she has been taken yesterday. She hopes this is somewhat a good thing, but just can't understand.

They come to one of the other doors and Christa gets a huge smile across her face and then throws her small body in front of the door with her arms stretched across so Mitch and Tara can't open it up to put one of the women in there for safe keeping. Mitch asks Christa what the hell she is doing and to move her skinny ass out of the way. Mitch just wants to lock these women in so she can get something to eat and some rest after a long two days on the road before going back to work. Mitch asks what's in the room or what has happened in the room. Christa yells out to both of them, "I have a surprise for you both, I did it myself, all by myself for you!" Mitch tells the two women they have taken to drop to their knees and leans them face forward into the wall. Mitch then shoves Christa out of the way and opens the door and flips on the light in the first room to find a strange woman chained to the wall. The woman is trying to see who has come in but is blinded by the bright light for a couple of minutes. Tara looks in the room and can't believe what she is seeing, then looks over at Christa and asks her if she has fucking lost her mind. Mitch stands over the woman with her back to Christa and her face turns red and her veins start to protrude on her forehead as her blood pressure goes up. Mitch closes her eyes and takes a deep breath trying to calm down. She turns to Christa and smiles, "So look what you did, all by yourself." Mitch walks over to Christa and gives her a hug and then kisses her on her forehead. Mitch has her hands on Christa's upper arms lightly and tells her what a good job she has done. Christa is beyond happy as she looks back at Mitch; she's so ecstatic that Mitch is happy and not upset with her. Mitch looks up from Christa and tells the women on their knees to get up to their feet. They place one of them in the room with the lady Christa has taken, retying her hands in front of her and taking out the gag from her mouth and taking her blindfold off too. As the blindfold comes off, the jogger woman can see them again, she starts to beg to be let go and tears roll down her eyes as she looks around the small prison of a room and sees another lady chained to the wall. Mitch looks at them both and smiles, “At least you’ll have someone to talk to in here.” Tara brings in a few bottles of water and sets them on the floor. “We’ll see you two pretty ladies soon.” Tara says, as they walk out and lock the door and shut off the lights. They take the other college woman to the next room and do the same thing. The new woman sees another young woman chained to the wall with her burns on her chest and her hand bandaged up with dried blood all over her. The woman starts to fight back, but she just can’t over power the three ladies. “Now now, don’t try and fight, it's pretty useless here and it will only make things worse for yourself. I'm glad you're here, feel free to ask her what happened to her." Mitch says to the new woman with a big evil smile. "Don't get to frisky with each other, save some for us too. " Tara says to the two captive animals. Tara blows them a kiss right before she shuts and locks the door while turning the lights out. The two women start to scream, which sets off a chain reaction in the other room, more screaming from the other two in the first room. Mitch loves the sounds of terror; she stands there for a moment, shuts her eyes and just listens to the blood curdling screaming, almost as if those sounds have transported her to heaven. The girls go upstairs making sure everything is secure as they walk up and out of the basement dungeon area.

Chapter 16

Mitch ask the girls to meet in the kitchen so they could all talk about Christa's reasoning to take that young woman all on her own, and not even talking to them about it. Everything is to be done as a team so they are all on the same page on what's going on, when, where and the hows. The girls go into the kitchen and sit at the table, Mitch sitting at the head of the table.

"Christa, did anyone see you out and about? Where did you take her from?" Mitch asks.

Christa replies, "No, no one saw me, I was super careful, looking around making sure and she was walking on the side of the highway, she was hitchhiking. I just asked if she needed a ride, she jumped in the car and that was it. No fighting or anything. Once she was in the car I pulled out a gun, and that was that, no big deal, really it wasn't, it was easy peasy." Tara just shakes her head and looks down at the table in disbelief.

"You took a really big risk with all the cameras and video everywhere now, you can't just go out on a whim and do whatever you want to do when it comes to this shit. I'm not going to prison because you're fucking high on drugs and thinking you can do anything you want Christa!" Tara says in a depressed but angry tone. "Ok let's not get crazy about this you guys, let's just get some rest and move forward tomorrow. Christa, it was really brave and wonderful what you did for us." Mitch said. Mitch walks over to Christa and leans in and gives her a kiss on her head as she strokes her hair a little bit. Mitch then fixes a scotch on the rocks and says goodnight to them and starts to walk away, but she stops, turns and looks at Tara. "Would you like to join me upstairs?" Mitch asks Tara. Tara puts her head up slowly and gets a half-cocked smile on her face, she doesn't answer Mitch, and she just gets up and follows her to her room. Christa yells out a goodnight to them and just hangs out in the kitchen for while with the television on.

"I'm glad you came up to my room Tara, shut the door. We need to talk about Christa and how fucked this is for all of us. I just wanted her not to worry about anything so that's why I didn't get too upset about it right now, but I'm pissed off. She could end all of this, be the end of us. I'm with you, and I'm not going to jail. I also don't want anything to happen to you Tara, I really care about you, I'll protect you anyway I can, no matter what it takes. Christa is a part of this family we have here but I do have an idea on what I'd like to see happen with this. I just need to know if your all in Tara, because if your not, it will be just a big mess, well more than it is now for sure. Let me think it over a couple days first then I'll have more of a plan for Christa. I just need some sleep right now, as I know you must too, we both work tomorrow, so lets get some rest and try not thinking about it. We did really well together, so let's just think about that right now and go off to dream land about it, thinking about having four women locked away just for us to play with. Now that's a nice dream to me." Mitch said to Tara.

Chapter 17

A couple of days passed by and Tara and Mitch have been going to work and doing their normal routine as people do in the world. Mitch has been giving much thought about Christa and how she wants to handle the situation at hand for just taking a woman on her own with no plan, thought or worry about them and their lives. Mitch gets angry every time she thinks about it, like her blood is going to just boil over and bubble out of her eyes.

Mitch calls everyone down to the area in the basement where the women are. Tara gets down there first and Mitch just tells her to follow her lead and not to worry about anything. Christa is the last one down and is her happy go lucky self. Mitch pulls out a joint and lights it up, puffing from it then hands it to Christa. Christa gets a huge smile on her face and takes the joint from Mitch without question. "Glad to see you loosen up a little Mitch." Christa says. Right as Christa is taking a big puff off of the joint, Mitch grabs Christa and throws her backwards into the chair and holds her there. Tara is a little taken back by this and just stands there and is stunned for a few seconds, then comes around and runs over and starts strapping Christa down in the chair. The burning joint falls to the ground and Christa starts screaming at them to stop, telling them this isn't funny. After a bit of a struggle Mitch and Tara get Christa secured sitting in the chair. Her arms fastened to the arms of the chair, and each leg is fastened to the front wooden legs of the chair by leather straps. You can hear the leather squeak as Christa tries to pull and tug on the straps to get out of them, but she can't. Mitch looks at Christa and just smiles at her. Mitch asks her how it feels to be strapped down and have no freedom left, to be at the mercy of friends. Christa looks at both of them for a few seconds and then starts to laughs, she just busts out a huge laugh. "Oh my God you guys, you got me, real funny. I get it, your teaching me a lesson. Point taken, come on you guys, I get it, I get it. I will never mess around on my own again, I promise. Whew, you guys had me going there, shit!" Christa says to them while still having a light laugh in her voice. Just then Mitch and Tara walk out of the room without saying a word and turn the lights off and shut the door. Christa yells out to them, "Nice, in the dark now for awhile I guess, ok no problem."

Mitch and Tara are putting on their gowns, gloves and masks in the other room where they keep all their equipment, cleaning supplies and the like. It only takes three to four minutes from them to put that on and be ready. They open the door and turn the light back on in the room that Christa sits in, Christa watches them walk in with their gowns and masks on. She knows the only time they wear them is when they are about to have fun with one of the women they have taken. “Look you guys got me, this isn’t funny anymore, let me up, Mitch! Tara! Please don’t, I love you guys, I LOVE YOU!” Christa yells out to them as loud as she can, she knows that look in their eyes, she knows she is about to be nothing, to be tortured by her own friends and housemates. Christa takes this last moment in time she has and looks into Tara’s eyes and starts to tell her something. “Tara, listen to me, Mitch and I took you a long time ago from….” Before Christa could finish what she was saying, Tara grabs a small towel and some duct tape and shoves the small towel in her mouth and places duct tape over the towel and wraps it around her head twice to keep it secure. Tara barely looks her in the eyes when she shoved the towel in Christa’s mouth. Tara has a blank and distance look upon her face as she placed the tape around her friends head and mouth. Mitch has a look of relief on her face that Tara had shoved that in Christa's mouth when she did. Mitch takes a big deep breath in and the lets it out and is back to her normal self. Now Christa is trying to be quite but can't, her eyes open wide full of fear as she starts to cry, her nostrils are flaring up as she tries to breath only through her nose, her breathing is intense and labored as she knows what is about to happen to her. Christa just wished she could have gotten out that last thing to Tara, now she will never know. Christa thinks that would have saved her, if only Tara would have listened to her before putting that towel in her mouth. She can't believe this is how it's going to end, at the hands of people she trusted with her life. By people she truly loves and only wanted to make happy. Tears roll down her face, as she now knows the true and utter horror they have been doing to all those women over the years. The hurt that those families must have felt, are still feeling of the not knowing, never seeing a smile on their daughters face again. A sharp pinching pain brings Christa out of her thoughts as she sits there and can't do anything; Mitch has just clipped off her index finger. Christa tries to scream but is only heard as muffled moans coming from under that towel as her finger hits the floor. One by one Mitch cuts off Christa's fingers, one by one they hit the floor. Tara looks on and just can't believe that Mitch is doing this, but she knows it must be done, she does think maybe they could have just cut her throat or shot her in the head quickly. Tara loves Mitch so much and knows this is just for them, their protection, and their lives. Tara just watches as Mitch's eyes light up as each finger is snipped off from Christa's hands. Tara knows she must show Mitch she agrees with this decision so Tara picks up a scalpel blade number 12, which is normally only used for cutting open a body for an autopsy, she places the blade on Christa's left upper leg on top and slowly runs it down to the her knee cap. Christa's face is a bright red from trying to scream and breath but can't, the rest of her body is slowly turning a shade of light cream to a pale white as the blood is running from her hands to the floor. Mitch sits back and looks at Christa then leans up and kisses her forehead. While Mitch kisses Christa's forehead slowly and softly she cuts her throat and let's her bleed out quickly. Mitch tells Tara she couldn't keep cutting her up; she was family, a friend after all. Mitch walks out slowly in disappointment and takes her gown, mask and gloves off and just walks upstairs and outside to the sunlight of the day to feel the warmth of the sun on her face. Tara just stares at Christa's dead lifeless body slumped in the chair. Tara pulls the tape off from around her head and takes out the towel soaked in saliva from her mouth. Blood still drips from her hands and her throat slightly, like a slow leaking faucet that needs a washer replaced.

Chapter 18

Tara walks out of the room and into the hallway, she leans against the wall and slowly slides down the wall to sit on the ground placing her head in her hands. She just sits there thinking back about Christa for a while, her smile, and her craziness she had brought into the house. Tara cracks a warm smile and puts her head up and looks over at the doors housing the women they took.

She stands up and walks over to the door where the first woman is being kept; she unlocks the door and flips the light on. She looks at both of them huddled together in fear on the floor. Tara grabs the one that has had her left thumb cut off and whore burned onto her chest. Tara unsecured her and takes her out of the room shutting and locking the door behind her. Tara then secures the lady's hands behind her just incase she tries to fight back or anything. The young lady is taken into the room where Christa's body is sitting limp in the chair; blood pooled all over on the floor. The lady starts to struggle as she looks at Christa, "No NO NO!" The lady screams as she ties to fight back. Tara sits her down on the stool and turns her away from Christa's body. Tara tells her not to move and to listen very carefully to what she is about to say to her. "If you want to live, then you'll grow some balls, get it together and clean this mess up. I want you to clean up all the blood from the floor, the chair, wherever else you see it. I will leave you locked in this room alone, but you have to clean this up and be a good girl. No trying to get away bullshit, no trying to kill us. If you do what I ask, then we will let you live." Tara tells the lady in a calm reassuring tone. The lady asks if she will be let go if she cleans up. Tara smiles at her. "If you clean up and be good, and we will let you live. If you help us with the other ladies we have to and we have no problems out of you, I will let you go. Only after the other three ladies are gone, do you understand?" Tara asks her as she is gently rubbing the ladies shoulders to comfort her... The lady remains silent for a while then shakes her head yes. "Good girl." Tara says as she leans in and kisses her forehead. Before Tara unties her hands from around her back, she does go and pick up the tools and anything sharp left behind. She places them all in a big tray and carries the tray out to be cleaned by them. "Just to let you know, we will check you before you leave this room. If you try and take anything or hide anything we will kill you. Remember, you have to be good and do a good job." Tara just smiles at her after she unsecured her hands then locked the lady in the room alone with their mess to be cleaned.

The lady looks around the room and just can't believe what she is seeing. She feels so sick inside looking at Christa sitting there lifeless.

She tries to collect herself as best as she can. After she collects herself enough to even fathom what she is looking at, she then takes a big deep breath and tries to focus on getting out of this hell she is in. The young lady begins to clean up the blood from the floor. She keeps telling herself to be brave and to do a good job so they will let her go. At the very least she is hoping they won't hurt her anymore, maybe if she does a good job they will keep their word and not hurt her. She does the best she can alone in the room with a dead body in a death chamber built for fun. She only has use of one hand at this point as she struggles to clean up this horrific sight of a mess. She does have a lot of doubt though and thinks they will kill her anyway, but she has to try something to get out of this place she is in, a nightmare come true. What other option does she have now? She just wants to see her family again, she wants to live and not be cut to little bits by them.

Chapter 19

Tara walks out to find Mitch sitting on the front big wooden porch swing with her flask in hand. Mitch just stares out at the beautiful trees and fields filled with flowers. “Crazy isn’t it, sometimes you have to do funny things for love I guess.” Mitch says to Tara. Tara walks over and sits next to her on the swing placing her head on Mitch's shoulder. "What if that was me Mitch?" Tara asked in a whispered voice, "Would you have done the same thing to me too?" Tara asks. "No, I would never do that to you no matter what. You're different than Christa is to me. You're smarter then to just go out and do something foolish like that. Even if you did it for a surprise for me, you wouldn't just go off without a plan just grabbing someone. We have done that a lot together so I know you wouldn't fuck it up like she did, she fucked up everything we had here." Mitch replied. "Well we don't know that she fucked it up either, but I know it didn't feel right for sure." Tara said with a big sigh that she didn't even realize she had let out while sitting there.

Tara lets Mitch know about the deal she made with one of the ladies in the basement. Mitch just got a really huge smile and laughed out loud with delight. Mitch shakes her head up and down and just thinks this is the best idea ever. Mitch even thinks she can make her into a pet of some sorts if it works. Tara does explain to Mitch that she thinks the best way to approach this is to be nice to the young lady, to be extra kind to her but with a firm hand. If they treat her well and reward her, this might just work out for them, then she can clean up all their messes. "We will have to figure something out about the sharp toys; we can't have her getting a hold of those, or even the non-sharp toys. It has been awhile now so we should go and check on her to see how she is doing down there. Christa needs to be put in a hole too." Tara tells Mitch. Mitch just stares off for a bit but agrees it has to be done, no time like the present. They get up from the swing and head downstairs while exchanging loving looks to one another as they walk inside.

Tara and Mitch open the door to check on the young lady cleaning up. Even though she only has use of one of her hands due to the pain from her previous injury she had received by them. The room looked pretty clean and smelled of bleach, things where put back in place neatly. The lady looks at them and asks if she has done a good job. After checking the room for a few minuets, they let her know it's not a bad job at all. "Looks pretty damn good in here for a gimp. Now we are going to get rid of Christa's body, we want you to help us, or at least see how we do it." Tara says. They get the old stretcher out with no wheels, just handles and lay it on the ground next to Christa's body. They place her limp body on the stretcher and tell the lady to go out first and down the hall so she can open the door down to the next level down inside the basement. The lady goes first as instructed and opens the door slowly, not knowing what to really expect. As the door opens the musty, decaying smell hits her nose, she covers her nose and mouth as she looks around and doesn't see anything but darkness before her. Tara tells her there is a light switch is on the right just inside of the doorway. The lady turns on the lights and sees a few short stairs leading down to a dry dirt floor area with a couple small mounds of dirt every foot or so along the dirt floor. She slowly walks down and steps aside so Mitch and Tara can get through with Christa's body. Mitch and Tara just look at each other then just pick up shovels and start to dig a hole for their friend, their family member that they had loved for so long. After some time digging, they walk up to the hole on the side and then just dump Christa's body in like anyone else they had thrown into a hole before. Mitch grabs a shovel and takes one last look at Christa then just starts throwing dirt on her body, eyes open staring blankly into the nothing that she now is while dirt is just being flung into the shallow grave. The young lady tries to pick up a shovel but Tara tells her not too, she will do it. Tara just told her to watch and learn how it's done. After about ten minutes of shoveling dirt the hole is filled and the shovels are leaned back against the brick wall. Mitch looks at the young lady and says, "That's it, that's all we do. Now we are going to take you back to the room ok? I also am going to take a look at the hand and clean it up for you." Mitch tells her in a soft solemn voice while caressing the young lady's face.

They open the door to the first room, there is another woman in there, and Mitch enters the room to unchain the other woman so she can move her into the second room. Mitch doesn't chain her up, just throws the other young woman in the room with the other two girls and locks the door. "What's your name by the way? Makes sense to know it at this point I guess." Mitch asks. The lady looks at her and can barely get out her name, she is still so very afraid and unsure of what to think at this point, she just wants to do whatever she can to stay alive and get out of this hellish nightmare she now finds herself in. "My name is Cindy." Said the young lady. "Well Cindy, I'm going to clean up and rebandage your hand up so it doesn't get infected. Now you are becoming one of us, we need you healthy and strong. Tara will go get you some food and something to drink, and will bring it down to you. Now I just want you to rest, you did a great job today." Mitch tells her with a big smile. "If you can help us for a while we can talk about getting your freedom back at some point, but if you fuck up, try to get away, try to hurt us, you're done. Got it?" Cindy shakes her head yes at Mitch while a new bandage is being placed on her left hand. Mitch kisses her on the forehead before she leaves Cindy behind and shuts and locks the door. She does leave the light on for Cindy. Tara brings her down a hamburger she made for her with mustard and some mayo on it along with two bottles of water and a small bag of chips. Cindy takes a big breath in when Tara leaves the room as she looks at her food and bites in. She is so hungry she just hopes its okay as she has been so starved for days that the burger tastes so good to her. Like the best hamburger she has ever had.

Cindy doesn't care what she needs to do, she just wants out of this freak show. That's all that she can think about now. She is in so much pain physically and mentally. Tears roll down her face as she eats wondering how she can trust any of this. How she can trust they will ever let her go at some point. She just tells herself to be strong and do whatever it takes. She drifts off to sleep after she eats just thanking God that the lights have been left on in this horrible dank chamber of a room.

Chapter 20

Mitch and Tara go through the next few days like everyone else, cleaning their house, going to work, shopping for milk or other needs. As Mitch has been going through her days she watches people more than she would normally. Looking at the young girl working the checkout counter at the store wondering, is she a murderer? Does she think about killing people, men, women, anyone? She looks at her co-workers wondering if they ever think the same thing. Mitch knows there has to be more people out there, lots more that live the same way that they do. How many people think about it intensely but never act on what they feel deep inside them? Mitch knows there's some sick fucks out there that rape and kill for fun, the backwoods type or bubbas as she calls them. She doesn't care or wonder about them, that's just their life for them. She ponders the everyday people you talk to, you wave at as you walk down the street. What lies inside of the basements or attics that line the boring everyday streets of town in nowhere USA? What do they look for in a kill? Why do they do it? Mitch doesn't know why she is thinking about it, she just knows she can't seem to get it off her mind these past few days. She thinks maybe because Christa is gone and that they did that to her, not some creepy shadow killer, but by there own hands. Mitch wants to truly feel bad, but she still got such rush out of it inside at first. She knows she has a heart because she cut her throat to end it quickly, but wonders why she can't feel it now. She just shakes her head for a bit and takes a deep breath to let it go. She knows there must in fact be more people like them out there, somewhere.

Mitch calls Tara on her cell phone from work to tell her she is going to take a few vacation days off from work. Tara agrees that this is a good idea and tells her she will call into work to take at least a couple of days off as well.

They need to relieve some stress they both have been feeling but not talking to each other about it. Mitch pauses on the phone and then utters out softly but fast to Tara, "I love you". Tara responds back softly to Mitch with a thank you and I love you too. Mitch hangs up the phone and heads into her boss's office to ask for a few days off. Mitch's boss waves her in his office and asks what he can do for her. Mitch explains she would like to take a few days off. He laughs and says, "You never take days off Mitch." He smiles and looks it up for her, "Wow!" He says. "You have five weeks available to take, you sure you only want a few days?" "Yeah, just a few days for me would be great, thanks." "You bet Mitch, I don't know what I would do without you sometimes. I need more people like you that don't call off or take time off, you're always on the job." Mitch's boss says then hands her paper work for her time off. Mitch takes the paper work nods and walks out of his office.

Diana rolls out in front of Mitch in her chair from her cubical. "So are you ever going to call me Mitch?" Diana asks with a stern but pouty look on her face. Diana grabs the paper work from Mitch's hand. "Taking a few days off huh? Maybe I can help you out if you need anything while you're off." Diana says to Mitch as she hands back her paper work. Mitch grabs her arm and leans in close, and tells her to come with right now! Diana follows Mitch into a small storage room at the other end of the building. Mitch asks her what her problem is, she tells her she doesn't want anyone at work to know about them fucking. Before Diana can answer Mitch grabs her by the back of her hair and pulls her in for a long passionate kiss. As Mitch thrusts her tongue in Diana's mouth and kisses her slowly, Mitch slides her other hand up her skirt and down her panties that are already getting wet from Mitch's intense kiss. Mitch starts teasing Diana's clit by lightly touching it with her fingers, putting her finger inside her then teasing her clit again, back and forth she does this making Diana want to be fucked badly and passionately. Mitch stops kissing her and looks her in the eyes, "Is this what you want, you want me to fuck you?" Diana starts to beg Mitch to fuck her as she is pawing at Mitch's clothes. "Please Mitch, please give me what I want." She whispers. Mitch grabs her and turns her around so she is facing away from Mitch. Mitch then spreads her legs apart with her feet as Mitch pushes her facing down on a wooden cabinet.

Mitch rips her panties down a few inches and starts slowly finger fucking her from behind. As Mitch is fucking her with her fingers she pushes her body into her then back out as if she is fucking her with a cock, Diana starts to moan and scream out. Mitch covers her mouth with her hand and tells her quietly but violently to shut the fuck up and take it like the no good whore she is. Diana can't take it, she starts to orgasm hard and her body begins to shake and quiver, barely able to remain standing. Mitch feels her clit swell on her fingers as she orgasms and whispers, "That's a good whore." into Diana's ear. Mitch moves her finger around a bit on the top of her clit, or the pearl, making her climax even more until she can't anymore. "My sweet fucking whore." Mitch whispers to her as she brings up her two fingers she just used to fuck her with and sticks them in her mouth to be licked clean. Diana moans softly as she tastes her own juices from her pussy. “Mmm.” Mitch then grabs Diana and turns her around fast and firm holding her by her upper arms tightly and tells her, “Don’t ever fuck with me, and don’t ever bring anything up at work about us fucking, ever!” Diana just looks at her and says she is sorry. Diana is so turned on by Mitch being so rough and violent, she asks Mitch for more, Diana is wet and longing for more from Mitch. Mitch wipes her hand off on Diana’s blouse and just leaves her in the storage room shaking and out of breath. Mitch is off to enjoy her few days off with Tara. Diana is just left yet again wanting more of Mitch, so she locks the door and pleasures herself thinking about Mitch raping her and yelling at her violently, calling her a whore.

After Diana gets her self off, she tries to pull herself together and freshens up in the restroom before going back to her cubical. When she gets back to her cubical she looks up Mitch's home address on her work computer and writes it down. Diana has access to personal files for emergencies or other work related reasons. She is going against work policy and puts Mitch's address in her purse in case she might just drop by to surprise Mitch, not knowing that she is with Tara or the horrors that lie behind the front door at Mitch's house.

Mitch leaves work, but after driving down the road for a while she just can't help but to pull off the road for a quick get off herself after finger fucking the woman at work. She needs a quick release from the build up of being so rough with her. Being rough and not having any warm blood to go with it. Mitch fantasizes about what had just taken place, only this time as Diana is climaxing, Mitch takes out her knife and guts her from behind, Diana never sees it coming, no matter how she tries to get away she can't, she quickly dies as her intestines spill out onto the floor in front of her. Mitch gets off quickly and intensely on this thought and right then she orgasms. Her hand is shaking and she just starts laughing out loud. She sits there for a few moments to collect her self before getting back on the road to go home and start her vacation. Mitch just relaxes for a moment thinking about gutting Diana as she fucks her. Mitch thinks this would be a great way for her and Tara to bond more in their relationship. Both of them fucking one of the girls they have and letting their guts fall on to the floor so they would be able to see their own horror of a death right before them as they come to climax as they die.

Chapter 21

Mitch walks into the house to find Tara in the kitchen making some early dinner for them. “Well, I called work and got four days off to be with you and our little projects.” Tara says with a half-cocked evil grin. Mitch smiles back and tells her that she needs to wash up real quick.

Tara walks over and kisses Mitch on the lips. Mitch gently pulls away and goes to wash up before Tara can slip her soft tongue into Mitch's mouth. She doesn't want Tara to smell or taste Diana on her. Mitch doesn't know why she keeps falling prey to this other woman at work. She cares for Tara, doesn't she? Mitch is getting so confused about everything that has happened in the past couple of weeks, she knows she just needs to have a drink and relax. Mitch runs up stairs to shower and change before dinner. Tara watches Mitch run up the stairs and wonders why she just couldn't take one moment to kiss her. Tara wants to make love to Mitch so badly, give Mitch her blood and pain. Mitch is very much a sadist, and Tara being a masochist makes them a great couple in the works. Tara stands there for a few moments fantasizing about Mitch taking her and making small cuts on her breasts, then licking the blood off. Just this very small thought of this makes Tara's pussy wet and wanting Mitch.

Tara goes into the kitchen and takes dinner off the stove then runs right upstairs and into Mitch's room. Tara has brought a small knife from the kitchen with her and starts to undress in the bathroom. She calls out to Mitch right before she enters into the shower with Mitch. Mitch turns around, slightly startled, and sees Tara standing before her with the knife in hand. Tara is slowly running the blade tip up and down her body teasing Mitch, and herself. Mitch grabs Tara and pulls her in closer while taking the knife from her hand. Mitch goes in and gives her a deep and passionate long wet kiss. Tara gives in easily wanting Mitch so badly. Their naked wet bodies together, Mitch pushes her gently back a bit and cuts Tara's right breast slightly, she just watches the blood mix with the water and start to run down Tara's body. Tara is so excited by the burning pain of the cut. She starts to touch herself as Mitch continues to cut more. Cutting deeper on the other breast, exposing some breast tissue, Tara screams out in pain and pleasure as the water hits her new deep cut. Mitch grabs and squeezes her breast tightly, Tara screams and moans for more. Mitch slowly drops to her knees and starts licking and kissing Tara's pussy as the blood just runs down on her face. Mitch can taste Tara, her juices mixing with the hot water as Mitch sucks on Tara's clits making her climax with excitement, Tara moans as she is grabbing at the walls in the shower trying to hold herself up as she becomes weak in the knees. Slightly shaking and heart racing, she drops to her knees and throws her arms around Mitch and just kisses her like she has never kissed her before, enjoying the taste in Mitch's mouth before they get out of the shower and continue with their day. Mitch just makes sure she has given Tara total pleasure because she does feel a little guilty about fucking the other woman earlier. Mitch just wishes that Tara wasn't so into pain, she would like her to fear a little more, to be able to give her more fear and painful screams, Mitch being a true sadist, like a cat wanting to trap a mouse before the kill.

After dinner they both go down stairs to the lower basement area and to the door where Cindy is. They have been treating her well the last few days by bringing her water and good food while just barely giving anything to the other three young women they have locked in the other room together. Tara opens the door and greets Cindy with a smile and a warm hello. "Well it's time to earn your way out of here. Sorry it's been a few days, probably feels like forever for you down here. For the most part we will give you free rein with us but we will be keeping you on a leash as it where, but you're here to help us out now. Just remember don't even try to fuck with us; you'll be dead before you even realize it."

Tara has Cindy come into the room where she had cleaned up before and sees one of the women secured to the metal embalming table with a towel in her mouth so she can't talk or yell out. Tara explains to Cindy that most of the time they would have already cleaned her up before bringing her into this room, but since there are three women in one room it's not the best option right now. "Normally they would be showered before being brought in here, but for now we will just use a hose and clean her off somewhat as she is lying on the table. This table is made for embalming so it does have a working drain we hooked up for water and blood to go down the drain. This hose is hooked up to both hot and cold water so we will make sure its warm. Here are some gloves for you to put on. As you can see we also would normally wear the full surgical gowns and masks like Mitch has on but you won't really be needing one, I won't wear one either for this I guess. Also I don't want you to start freaking out on what you see, because it's not for everyone. If there is something you just cannot handle, just suck it up and deal with it. Here is a table of tools that we use.” Tara flips back a blue thin towel to reveal a scalpel, pliers, hammer, clamps and three retractors to show them to Cindy. “Again we will be watching you closely around everything. Ok any questions?” Cindy just looks at Tara and Mitch with a look of shear terror and just shakes her head no. “Ok no questions. Good. Glad to see you are paying attention.” Tara said with a cheerful but stoic expression.

“Turn on the water to make sure it is nice and warm for her then get started cleaning her up a bit.” Says Tara. Cindy turns on the water and lets it run until she feels it’s a good temperature. She just can’t believe what is happening, where she is and why she is now helping them. She just feels so sick inside but she tells herself to just keep it together and get through this. They will see that I can do a good job and are like them so they will let me go, she tells herself inwardly. Cindy picks up the hose and walks over to the young woman lying strapped down to the table and starts hosing her off. The woman tries to scream while looking right at Cindy, thinking maybe she will help her. The woman on the table knows she is just like her, taken against her will and must surely know that this too will also happen to her when they are done with her. Cindy tries hard not to look the woman in the eyes, just keeping her head down washing her up with soap and water. "Okay that's good enough for me." Mitch tells Cindy. Cindy slowly walks the hose back over and shuts the water off, as she does her hand begins to shake. She doesn't know what to expect. All she does know is that it isn't going to be good at all, after cleaning up that horrible mess a few days ago and placing a human in the ground never to be seen again. How they treated her too, cutting her thumb off, burning “whore” into her chest. Looking at these two monsters that look just like regular good people, she just can’t believe it. She just keeps telling herself over and over, get out of this alive! No matter what they did to me, treating me like just a piece of meat.

Mitch calls Cindy over to the opposite side of the table from her. “Ok, if I need your help I’ll let you know.” Tara is standing back watching, making sure Cindy doesn’t try anything. Keeping Mitch safe. Tara does have a loaded gun in a holster in the back of her waistband hidden in her jeans. Just then Mitch looks at Cindy and takes her good hand in hers. “I’m so happy you’re with us now and I’m so very sorry for what we did to you.” Mitch then takes her hand and kisses it over the mask she has on. Mitch just wanted to reassure her. "Just to let you know when we found this one, she was coming down a trail from a small mountain area, that's why her body looks so good and tone. I can't help it, I have a thing for hot strong women, right Tara?" Says Mitch.

The whole time the lady is just laying there, helpless, trying to struggle to get away but can't move but an inch. She's trying to ask Cindy for help but it only comes out as muffled sounds and moans, nothing that anyone can make out. She does gag on it from time to time, but it's like she not even in the room. They don't even pay her any mind, like she's not a person lying there in need. As her calls for help are not received, the veins on her head and neck are protruding outward from all the force she is excerpting trying to scream out. Her eyes are blood shot and tearful. Her whole body shakes in fear of the unknown, as she lies there alone. She just can't comprehend what this is. She thinks about her life and how much it means to her, just life in general. I've studied hard and long to become a doctor, I'm not there yet but I'm on my way. I eat right and exercise and this is what I get! She screams in her head. As fear creeps in so deep as she looks upon Mitch's eyes over the mask. She just can't believe this is really happening.

Just then she feels something cold go up inside of her pussy, it shocks her right out of her thoughts. She tries to look but can't see what it is, all she knows its something cold and slippery. Mitch just watches as Cindy takes the handle of a metal knife and is slowly and gently fucking the woman with it. “That’s it, slowly in a bit and slowly out.” Mitch says. Cindy has a hold of the blade with a thick towel around it; Cindy also put a little bit of Vaseline on it for her. Ok, show her the knife, and then go back to fucking her slowly with it. Cindy does as Mitch asks; she shows the woman the knife with blade exposed and then goes back to fucking her pussy with the handle. Tara at this point does have her hand on her gun to be ready if Cindy tried to stab Mitch with the knife.

Mitch now places her hand around the woman’s throat and squeezes slightly with her hand. Fingers wrapped around her neck, slowly closing her hand tightly as she looks right into her eyes. After almost two minutes Mitch slowly loosens her grip around the woman’s throat and Mitch watches her face go from red, to pink and back to a nice fleshy pink color as she chokes trying to get any air back into her lungs. The woman's eyes went from white to blood red from the pressure around her throat.

Mitch tells the woman lying there in fear, since she is a runner that she has a little gift for her. Mitch picks up a large syringe filled with lidocaine and starts slowly injecting it into the woman's right upper leg just above the knee. She takes her time and moves around the whole leg to make sure it becomes numb just above her knee. While Mitch waits for the lidocain to take affect she asks Tara to put on some music for them. Mitch wouldn't normally numb someone before cutting them apart, but she wants the element of surprise for her.

Mitch has Cindy start fucking the woman with the handle of the knife and instructs her to make some cuts just on the outer part of her clit area on her pussy before she fucks her with the handle. Cindy's hand starts to shake and tries to make a cut but she just cannot bring herself to do it. Cindy asks Mitch to show her. Mitch takes the knife from Cindy's trembling hand and makes a few small cuts on the young woman's pussy just on the outer area, the cuts are small, three to four inches long and only about a quarter of an inch deep or so. As the cuts are being made the woman screams out in terror trying to say no, but you can't make out what she is trying to scream with the towel shoved in her mouth. She tries to wiggle and move her way out of being restrained to the table franticly as she screams and tries to call out for help. No matter how she tries she just can't move more than an inch and there is no way for her to get out of the straps that are holding her down to the cold metal table of gloom. You hear laughing as all this is going on, it's Tara, because she knows they haven't even gotten started yet. Tara is leaning backwards against a small table with her arms crossed watching them. She so loves seeing the blood too. Even though the cuts are small there is a lot of blood running down her pussy to her ass as she lies there, with her small-framed body trembling with fear.

Cindy just can't believe she is watching this happen and sitting there helping. She tries to show little fear but Tara and Mitch both know she is scared out of her mind right now, like they can almost see her brain spinning as she sits there at the ready. Mitch is just so happy that Cindy is trying and making a clear effort, that's all she can really ask for at this point. Mitch knows that you can make someone a killer, you can teach certain people to be bad even if they were not born that way. Mitch is more than happy to guide her through it and help her; it actually gets her a little excited at the thought of making a sexy new woman into a killer. A monster to unleash into the world, but she also knows this can take years, as she looks at Tara standing there as these thoughts run through her mind.

Mitch checks the right leg on the woman to see if it's numb at this point. She takes the needle and starts poking at her leg, she sees no change in the woman's face. No signs of pain so she believes that the leg is numb and ready. Mitch picks up a scalpel, number 10 blade and starts to cut into her flesh just above the knee, as she cuts she looks up again at the woman, still no signs of any pain. She cuts all away around the leg, the woman cannot see what is happening to her leg, and her head is slightly tiled back and strapped down. She can only feel some pressure around her leg. Mitch then picks up a small self-holding retractor and cuts down through the thin layer of yellow fat down to the thinner layer of muscle. Mitch keeps working her way around and through down to the bone, replacing retractors as she goes with larger ones so she can see what she is working on. She has no suction unit to keep the blood out of the way so she just keeps placing towels on and around the area to help soak up all the blood that is just pouring out of her leg. Mitch sees an artery that is a heavy bleeder, spraying all over. So she just clamps it off so the woman won't bleed to death before she can get her leg off and have more fun with her little toy.

Cindy is sitting there in almost a shock state watching this horror, the blood, and all the muscles moving and twitching from within. Cindy is a weird shade of pale gray, just frozen in fear.

Mitch sees the bone, the femur to be exact. “Aha, here we are.” Mitch says. Mitch picks up a crude yard hatchet. Now the woman can see the hatchet and starts screaming through the towel to please stop. No matter how she tries, she knows she is done in; there is nothing she can do. Not truly knowing what Mitch has already done to her leg because she couldn’t feel anything. Mitch raises the hatchet high, takes a good look at the spot to hit on the bone and with all her might swings the hatchet downward striking and breaking the bone. The bone is thick and tough to break with this crude tool. The bone is broken but not all the way through. Mitch takes another fast and heavy swing; you can hear the loud clank of the hatchet blade hitting the metal table right through the bone. With the woman in such a panic from hearing that loud crack and clank of metal on metal, she tries as she might but can not scream out through the towel or move at all but she tries. Mitch's eyes light up in delight and she picks up the lower half of the leg and shows it to the woman on the table. The woman's eyes open so wide it almost seems as if her eyes would pop right out. The woman stops failing around so much and begins to vomit at the sight of her leg or maybe she has gone into shock from all of this gruesome horror she has just endured. Mitch takes the towel out of her mouth so she doesn't choke on her own vomit and die. Vomit has already shot out of her nose before the towel came out. At the sight of all this happening at once, Cindy passes out and hits the floor, falling right off the chair. Mitch takes a drill and starts to drill hole after hole into the woman's chest, the woman isn't screaming anymore, she is in shock from the loss of blood and pure pain that has happened to her body at this point. Mitch gets five holes through her chest when the woman starts to shake for just a moment then just simply goes limp, nothing, no movement anymore. She lies on the table dead, blood still dripping onto the floor. The smell of vomit fills the room. There is silence in the room for a few moments, Mitch always gets quite when they die, because it's all over, her excitement and fun has now passed.

Mitch takes her mask off and goes over to Cindy lying on the floor. Mitch shakes her. Nothing, she's out cold. Mitch tells Tara to get her some water, Tara hands Mitch a bottle of water. She opens the bottle and pours it on Cindy's face, Cindy starts to move and her eyes open slowly as she wakes up. Mitch helps Cindy sit up on the floor and starts to gently rub her back and asks if she is ok. Cindy still unsure of her surroundings for a few seconds starts to come around and shakes it off. She looks up at Mitch smiling at her, she utters out in a shaky voice, "I don't think I can do this for you, I don't think I have it in me. I just don't want to die, please Mitch. Spare me." Mitch just keeps her smile on her face and helps Cindy to her feet. Mitch tells her to take it easy and don't worry. "This is your first time to see such things. It's not easy for everyone but I want to help you get there. If you just don't want to get there with us, then yes, we will kill you. Take the night to think about it, take your time and really think about what you really want. You can help us, you can learn to kill or you will be tortured and die, never to be found again. Either way you decide its ok with us. I don't want you to do anything you don't want to do from this point on." "I don't want to be here!" Cindy says to them with some force. Mitch places a finger over her mouth to be quite, and tells her it's too late for that. "You are here now, there is only two ways out of this now, sorry but that's life sometimes. You have to make choices, hard ones, life isn't easy but there is always a way, in this case you have two ways out. It's up to you how you want to leave, walk out or in the ground." Mitch gives her a hug and walks her back to the last room down the hallway and tells her again, "Really think about what this is and where you now are." As Mitch walks her back to the room, she tell Tara to start cleaning up and that she will be back in a few minutes, that she wants to talk to Cindy alone. Tara just sighs and starts to clean up.

Mitch locks the door behind them both and just looks at Cindy as she just stands there in fear looking back at Mitch. Mitch walks up to her and holds her close and leans in and starts to kiss her on the lips. Mitch tells her not to be afraid and starts to kiss on her neck. Cindy abruptly blurts out she's not a lesbian. Mitch tells her to shush and that it's not about liking girls or not liking girls. "It's about sex and excitement and what I want. I'm not fucking you, I'm just kissing you, showing you I'm not here to hurt you but I would like to fuck you of course. That will happen, you will want to fuck me someday." Mitch just starts kissing Cindy again, and Cindy gives in to her, kissing her back gently and petting her. "I do think this should stay between us, we don't need to share everything with Tara right now, ok? Just take some time and I'll be back later to get your decision you have made, either way it will be ok." Mitch tells her. Mitch leaves out of the room locking the door behind her but leaving the lights on for Cindy once more. Cindy doesn't know what to think, she just wants to get away from them.

Mitch returns to the room and helps Tara clean up the room and take the body to be buried. Tara asks Mitch why she isn't having Cindy help them clean up. "I thought that was the point."

Mitch tells her it will happen but they have to take their time with her, it's all a new world she has never seen or probably hasn't wanted too. "We just need to take it slow with her, she will come around." Mitch tells Tara. After they clean up everything they go back upstairs to have a drink and spend some time together.

Chapter 22

Tara is in the kitchen making their drinks and hands one to Mitch. Tara asks what Mitch was doing in the room with Cindy. "What do you mean what was I doing in there? I was talking to her, reminding her of the two choices she has to choose between." Mitch responded. Tara then says, "It just seems you have taking a weird liking to her, I don't know. I thought we were going to try and date or whatever." Mitch walks over and stands behind her and rubs her shoulders and explains to Tara that she likes all the women they take, and that they don't take ugly women for a reason. "We are starting something new, but this is not new information to you, I like them and it excites me, but I love you Tara. It's you and me against them all, we are doing this together. Fucking them, dismembering them, killing them all together. This isn't going to work if you're getting jealous all the sudden on me." Tara shakes her head yes and agrees with her Mitch and tells her she is sorry for even bringing it up. She tells her she feels silly for even thinking anything and that she knows she loves her. Tara turns to her and kisses her slowly and passionately. Their breath tastes of whiskey as they kiss and touch each other. A car can be heard coming up the gravel driveway, they stop kissing and go to the window to see who in the world it could be coming to their farmhouse this late evening, it's nearing nine in the evening and no one ever comes out here.

All that can be seen out the window are headlights coming from the car as it gets closer and closer. Tara reaches for her gun but Mitch stops her. "Don't do that. We have no idea who it even is, let's not take it that far yet." As the car gets close to the end of the driveway a motion light comes on at the front of the garage now they can see the car. "Oh shit!" Mitch says. Tara asks in excitement, "Who is it?" Mitch tells her it's a woman she works with. "I can't believe she's here now." Mitch tells Tara to stay out of sight and stay low and to go upstairs to wait. "I'll explain later." Tara gets low and sneaks past the windows to the stairs and runs upstairs really fast but quietly.

There is a knock on the door and Mitch goes to open the door. It's Diana, the woman Mitch has been fucking from work standing right there on her front porch. Mitch opens the door and asks her why in the hell she is there and how did she even know where she lives. Diana just smiles and grabs Mitch and kisses her then pulls back and asks if this is a bad time. Diana can see Mitch is not happy at all. Diana asks Mitch if someone else is here and why she looks so mad, after all Mitch had just fucked her at work earlier with no issues about that. Mitch knows she has to try and just get rid of her. She is trying to make a go of it with Tara after all. Tara has already questioned her about Cindy and now this. Mitch feels so trapped for the first time in a long time. "Look this is a bad time you need to just go. I don't know how you got my address and I don't care right now, you just need to leave." Mitch tells Diana. Diana just stands there for a moment with a puzzled and hurt look on her face, and then she blurts out, "So I'm good enough to fuck but nothing else? Fuck you Mitch!" Then she turns and walks quickly in huff back to her car and drives away down the long dirt and gravel driveway blowing up dust as she speeds away.

"Ok she's gone Tara, you can come back down now." Tara walks down the stairway slowly just glaring at Mitch. Tara asks Mitch why she came and what was going on. Tara was after all, listening to their conversation and is hoping Mitch will come clean and be honest with her. She loves Mitch so dearly and can't bare the thought of her being with someone other than her right now. The only time when it doesn't matter is when they are together with a woman they have downstairs, that's a given for them and the only time that fucking someone would be acceptable now, at least in Tara's mind. Even that isn't easy for her to think about now either. Tara is waiting for an answer and just stands there at the bottom of the stairs looking into Mitch's eyes. She can tell Mitch is nervous and is searching for something to say. This is the first time she has seen Mitch at a loss for words and being so fidgety. Mitch utters out quietly, "I have fucked her a couple of times, she means nothing and it was before we started hooking up." Tara just shakes her head in disappointment and tells Mitch she can't believe she is standing there looking her straight in the eye lying to her. "I heard what you two said from upstairs you know, you just fucked her today. Today Mitch! If I can't trust you to just to tell me the truth about a woman what else can't I trust you with? Everything we do involves total trust, we can't have secrets Mitch. We need to keep it open and honest here or this, everything we have here, will fall apart. We trust each other enough to kidnap women, kill them in our own home and trust that no one will say anything ever, but you can't just tell me the truth about fucking some woman. Nice Mitch, real fucking nice!" Tara remarks. Tara walks away and leaves Mitch just standing there. Mitch doesn't say a word and just walks in the kitchen to get her drink.

Tara walks downstairs into the basement and opens the door to the room that holds the two women. Tara pulls out her gun and shoots one in the head, no drawn out killing or tortures no screaming or sorrow, just shoots her as she sits on the floor. The woman slumps over motionless, the other woman starts screaming and freaking out. Tara shuts and locks the door behind her. The woman that was shot didn't even have a chance to realize what happened, she was lucky, just a quick clean kill.

Mitch hears the gun shot from the kitchen and drops her drink from her hand the glass hits the floor and smashes into tiny bits all over the tile floor. Mitch runs downstairs in a panic and sees Tara standing there in the hallway with her gun in her hand. "What did you do?" Mitch yells out. "I made it right, since you felt the need to lie to me about something like that when we have all this to worry about. I just went ahead and put a bullet in her brain, now she's gone, no pleasure for you Mitch." Mitch just looks at both the doors and in a panic and she runs over to the door with the girl she has been training and starts to open it. Tara tells Mitch not to worry, it wasn't her she shot. It was one of the other women. Mitch takes a deep sigh of relief that it wasn't her pet in training. "All that we went through to get these women and you just blow one of them away, just end it fast like that, what the hell is wrong with you Tara!" Mitch screams out. Tara just throws Mitch an evil smile and says, "Now we are even for you lying to me, just keep it real Mitch, always just be honest with me and we will not have any problems. I know I might have to sleep with one eye open now. You took Christa without any thought. You could just as well do the same to me. Isn't funny how one little lie can change everything Mitch?" Tara then places her gun in her holster and walks out and back upstairs leaving Mitch with the mess. "Clean up your own messes Mitch." Tara says as she walks out.

Mitch opens the door to see what Tara has truly done and sure enough she sees one of the women slumped over on the floor with a bullet right through her forehead. It was the college girl they had taken together, Mitch just looks at her beauty and shakes her head. "What a fucking waste, damn it!" Mitch says under her breath. The other woman in the room that Christa took has pushed herself into the corner as far as she can go to get away from Mitch. The woman whispers in a low tone while crying,

"Please don't kill me, please, whatever you want I'll do it, just don't kill me." Mitch just looks at her and tells her to be quite. Mitch grabs the dead girl by her ankles and drags her out of the room leaving a trail of blood behind on the cement floor, like a dirty mop. She gets the body out of the room and shuts and locks the door behind her. She leaves the lights on so the other woman will just be sitting in the room watching the blood and bits of brains all of the wall dry like paint, to wait and wonder what will be her fate.

Outside of the room in the hallway Mitch drags the body over to the other set of stairs to go down to bury her. Before Mitch takes her down, she sits on the ground with her and puts her body against hers. The dead girls head up close on her chest, Mitch just sits there and strokes her beautiful long brown hair and kisses the side of her face. Mitch tells the dead girl that she would have been so great, so beautiful to lovingly take apart slowly, now you're just gone. "When I saw you at the restaurant I just knew you would be a great screamer, a fighter. Now you just lay here with no beating heart no movement or fear." Mitch pulls the girls shirt up to her neck and caresses her breasts and feels her thin tight tummy. Mitch is just so saddened by this waste of a beauty, the time it took to take her. The worry of being caught in the motel was just all a big horrible waste. Mitch then just shakes her head and hits her fist against the wall hard. She stands up and grabs the girl and throws her down the stairs to the bottom in the musty dirt. Mitch digs a hole and throws the girl in there, as she shovels dirt on her body she wonders how this will all get back to normal for them, or would it ever be the same again? Tara has never been out spoken like that before or even threatened to do anything that would hurt their friendship over the years they have known each other. Once the body is covered she puts down the shovel and goes upstairs.

Mitch goes over to the door where Cindy is being kept, she places her hand on the door with her head down just thinking. She wants to go in and be with her, be close to her, give her pain to ease her own. Mitch puts her head up and just grabs a mop and cleans up the blood that was left in the hallway. Mitch doesn't clean up the blood in the room from where the girl had been shot only in the hallway. Blood fills the bucket of water as Mitch mops and rings out the mop head. Mitch whispers to herself, "I'm getting to old for this shit." She puts everything back in its place and locks everything down and slowly walks up the stairs to the main house.

Chapter 24

Sun light comes in through an upstairs bedroom hitting Mitch right in the face. Mitch's eyes open but she squints as the warm light hits her face. She rolls over and sees that it is later then she has ever slept, the house is very quite. Mitch gets out of bed and goes to get ready for the day by jumping in a hot shower, she lets it run over her body as if it will wash away last night somehow. She thinks she should have just told Tara about the woman from work, but how do you just blurt that out to someone you're trying to make a real relationship with? Mitch just wants to stay in the shower so she doesn't have to even go down to see Tara, she doesn't want any fighting or bitching. She just wants it to go back to the way it was.

Tara is down stairs making breakfast for both of them as she hears the shower running and knows Mitch is awake. Tara has been up for awhile already and has fed and watered the women downstairs and cleaned the house too. Mitch comes downstairs into the kitchen and doesn't know what to say to Tara. "Good morning Mitch, I'm making breakfast so just sit down and it will be ready in a bit." Tara tells Mitch. Mitch sits down at the table and is surprised Tara is being so nice to her this morning. Tara brings over a cup of coffee to Mitch and sets it in front of her. Mitch smiles and says thank you. She looks out the kitchen window at the wonderful landscape outside of their house, just staring out not wanting to say anything so she doesn't say anything wrong. Tara sets down two plates full of food for her and Mitch, eggs sunny side up, bacon and some toast with butter and huckleberry jam on it. Tara just smiles at Mitch and then leans over and turns on the small television that is on the kitchen table. "Let's see what's going on in the world and it will give us some noise so this awkward silence can be broken for Gods sake already. Let's just put yesterday behind us Mitch and move on. We need to stay strong together to make this work like it always has. I care and love you very much Mitch, even if we don't work out we need to be able to always keep going as friends, or more like family. We are all we have in this world, I don't want it to get fucked up just because of some woman came knocking at our door." Tara said sweetly to Mitch. Mitch shakes her head in agreement with Tara and starts to eat her breakfast. Tara has a great idea to have a small picnic by the pond and go for a walk in the woods since they are off from work for a few days. She doesn't tell Mitch, she thinks this will be a nice and happy surprise for Mitch.

Turtles sit on rocks in the sun with heads held high, a slight wind blows through the wild flowers and fish can be seen swimming in the pond. Tara has a nice blanket set up next to the pond, the blanket has two wine glasses and a bottle of cheap wine chilling in a bucket of ice. Tara texted Mitch to meet her out by the pond at 12:30 pm and it was approaching that time and no sign of Mitch yet. All of the sudden to hands come down onto Tara shoulders out of nowhere. Tara is visibly startled and turns quickly and franticly and she grabs the person's arm but as she looks she sees it is Mitch standing crouching down behind her. Tara yells out in a fun voice, "Shit bitch you scared me to death almost!" Tara is relieved it's Mitch. Mitch looks at everything and sits down with Tara on the blanket; Tara pours them both a glass of wine. They lay there talking and laughing for an hour, and Mitch tells her this is just great and relaxing, something she really needed. Just to let everything go and glad they are taking some time to go to a happy good place she hasn't been to in a long-long time, year's maybe. " I feel like we are in a better place than we where yesterday for sure, this has been just such a great time Tara, thank you, I really needed this and to be with you now is wonderful." Mitch tells Tara. Tara starts cleaning up the picnic area and tells Mitch it's time to go have a little more fun now in the basement. Mitch's face lights up and helps Tara pick up everything and they walk back to the house hand and hand laughing and talking, like two teenagers in love sneaking around from their parents.

Chapter 25

Arriving back to the farmhouse they leave the basket by the door and head downstairs to the hidden second basement area for fun. Could this day be any happier for them at this point? They are truly the happiest they have been since Christa has been there. She was the one who always brought craziness and fun to the house, the life of the party. Tara was worried they may never get back to where they should be, but she thinks this is a great start for sure, small step but every step is one to coming back and being whole again, for both of them. Bringing back some part of their normal that most people would surely cringe at if they knew the horrors in theirs minds and on their property.

Once downstairs Tara stops Mitch and asks what she wants to do with the young woman she is trying to train, trying to change into one of them. Tara apologizes again for walking in and shooting the college girl in the head and wasting her. Mitch goes in and hugs Tara and tells her its ok and all is forgiven. Tara continues to ask Mitch if she wants to keep the young woman for cleaning up and to show her or to just have fun and put her back into the mix for fun, sex and torture. As Mitch is thinking over all the pros and cons of keeping her around verses killing her, she walks into the storage room and starts placing tools, knives and gloves on a small tray to take into the torture room.

"I'm just not sure right now what I want to do with her, I would like to keep her but I don't want it to become a problem for us." Mitch tells Tara. "Why would that be a problem?" Tara asks. Mitch responds. "I just don't want you to think I'm keeping her around for the wrong reasons, that's all. I want to teach her, to see if I can teach her to be a killer, just to see if it's possible to turn someone into evil." "Well I don't see an issue with that. I don't think that would be a wrong reason as you say. I'm fine with it." Tara replies with a warm smile.

Mitch goes into the room where the woman is that Christa took to get her and move her into the fun room. As Mitch leaves the room Tara sets up her tablet off to the side in the room aiming it at the table where they will be strapping down the woman to kill. She places it quickly so Mitch won't notice it; she moves a few things around it to block it but making sure not to block the camera. Tara hits record and moves away from it as not to attract attention to it. Tara does a quick scan of the room so she knows where to be out of the way of the camera. Tara has been thinking about what Christa was trying to tell her before she died. What did that mean, Mitch and I took you when you were younger? Drunk? What did she mean? Tara wants to know and just wants a little video to hold over Mitch's head just incase. Tara is just getting pissed that Mitch doesn't want just her, like is just isn't enough. She also hopes that having the video will make Mitch tell her what Christa was going to say. Tara wouldn't use it against her for anything. She does truly love Mitch with everything she has.

Mitch walks the woman into the room with force and leads her over to the table, she tries to fight back but she is too weak from being under fed and not having very much water to drink as she was being held captive for well over a week long. Mitch asks Tara to help her get the woman on the table, but Tara says no, she will go get Cindy to help her. She tells Mitch she might as well keep helping and learning as they go. Tara goes and gets Cindy and tells her she needs to help Mitch with another woman and brings her into the room. Cindy goes over and helps lift the woman on to the table, Mitch tells her to start strapping down her arm and leg on her side. Cindy does as instructed while fighting against the woman to get her strapped down and secured. Mitch has her strapped down in mere moments but it takes Cindy minutes to get her strapped to the table. Once she is strapped down, Cindy tells them that it was way harder then she thought it would be, physically and mentally. Now strapped down, the woman is afraid and hopes it will be all over soon, this place will be gone, her worst fears coming true will all be over and she will soon be with her maker in his kingdom. Too weak to really fight or even scream out, she's just spent in everyway possible, she closes her eyes and just prays.

Mitch shoves a towel in her mouth just like the others to keep her screams or words to a low muffle. Mitch tells Tara to come on over and join in the fun. Tara smiles at Mitch and tells her, "No, that's ok. I want you to have all the fun on this one, I want to watch you teach and enjoy." Mitch's eyes just light up. Tara giving it all to her, all the pain, all the blood just for her. She thinks it's because she wasted the girl yesterday so she doesn't even give it another thought and gets to work on her.

Mitch picks up a small knife with a four-inch blade on it, and places the blade on the woman's sternum and slowly cuts into her flesh moving the knife carefully downward until she cuts to just between her breasts. The woman feels the burning from the cutting and tries to scream out but with the towel in her mouth and her throat being so dry from no water she can barely get anything out. She closes her eyelids tight but tears of pain still make their way out and run down the sides of her cheeks hitting the cold metal table. Mitch doesn't cut deep enough to do any real damage just enough to make some blood appear out from her flesh to see the reaction on Cindy's face. As she looks up at Cindy, she sees Cindy is taking it pretty well, she is a little pale but she makes a fake smile at Mitch to try and let her know, this is ok with me, I'm good with this. Mitch just chuckles under her mask and knows she is just trying to appease her at this point, but Mitch really believes she can change her and make her a monster inside. This wouldn't be the first Mitch has made a killer, she just wants to see if it can be done again, maybe the first time was just a fluke.

Mitch puts down the knife and picks up a scalpel but before she makes any cuts she explains to Cindy what she is about to do. Mitch tells Cindy that she loves the human heart and what it can do, how hard it works second after second it never stops until you are dead. All the different layers to get to it and how her big plan is to expose the human heart and have a woman live for days with her heart exposed. She hasn't done it yet, but keeps trying, how she loves to hold her hand on the beating heart to feel it keeping someone alive, and how fast it beats when someone is scared and their pulse rises. "It's my cocaine so to speak. So if you look at it one way, I don't torture people at all, I'm just looking for my drug, and not to kill them but to keep them alive with their chest opened and heart beating and thriving. That's exciting to me, that's what I focus on, but I know I have maimed some people in other ways, like you, your hand, your chest and taking a few of your teeth out. I don't know why, maybe I get sidetracked on other things, and I'm not alone, we all take part in this little process we like to call fun here." Mitch tells Cindy how beautiful she is with her scaring, now gimp hand.

Cindy just listened as Mitch explained her ways or her reasons; Cindy is just trying to keep it together while listening to this horrible woman. Cindy can't help think how she looks so normal, not like what you would think a monster would be. And Tara too, she is so pretty and nice. Cindy doesn't understand why they are this way or how they can do this and thinks it's just no big deal to kill people. These are living, breathing people. Sisters, mothers and daughters of someone out there just to be taking away and destroy everyone in this freak show academy.

Mitch decided to place an IV bag on the woman with normal saline in it, she wants to be able to keep a woman alive during this procedure as she calls it. The IV is placed and she has an extra bag to the side ready to go if needed. Mitch takes the ten-blade scalpel and makes an eight-inch cut just under her left breast to the side; she then makes another cut along the left side along her ribs. The woman again tries to scream and yell, and even move somewhat but to no avail, no one cares here and no one else can hear her. So again she just tries to be quiet, as she cannot give them the satisfaction of her pain as they cut her to bits. Mitch tells Cindy to come around and sit by her so she can help out, with a towel for the bleeding or anything else she needs. Cindy moves next to Mitch and does the best she can as she looks on at this horrible butchering that is going on right in front of her eyes. Mitch cuts through layer by careful layer until she reaches the ribs. She has Cindy using retractors to help keep the flesh pulled back so she can work. Mitch picks up an ordinary pair of garden shears and starts to cut the ribs out piece by small painful piece. After twenty minutes finally enough ribs have been cut away and there is blood everywhere. Cindy is trying to keep up with it but it's just so hard to deal with as she tries not to even look at what Mitch is doing. Mitch places a camping headlamp on around her head to be able to see into the dark open cavity better. Mitch looks in, there it is, there is her heart she wants so badly, look at it pump, just look at it, so wonderful and beautiful. Moving all the blood through and around to give her life with every beat. Mitch is just so into what she is doing she doesn’t notice anything going on around her.

Tara steps out of the room and goes into the storage area and fixes up a syringe with a small amount of anesthesia they have. She recaps the needle and places it in her pocket. Cindy noticed that Tara left the room but doesn’t think anything of it; maybe this is a normal thing that they do if one is just watching. Tara comes back into the room and goes over to the tablet and quickly turns off the camera that has been recording everything Mitch and Cindy have been doing in there. She again made sure she came at it from the side so she wouldn’t be recorded at all. Tara now just stands at the back of the room by the door just watching Mitch rip this woman apart, thinking about how much she loves her. She thinks about how easy it was for Mitch to be able to take Christa away from them, how easy it was to fuck some random woman from work and hide it. Tara knows she is a good person inside even though she has kidnapped, held captive and killed women too. She is still good inside she tells herself. Tara is getting more upset by the minute thinking about Mitch killing Christa. Watching her being so close and so happy showing Cindy how it's done. Tara knows she shouldn't feel so jealous, but she just can't help it.

Mitch now has her hand inside of the woman's chest and is touching her heart, she closes her eyes as she feels the heart beating in her hand, and it's her euphoria. Just then Mitch hears shuffling behind her of something coming to her from behind quickly but she is almost in a trance. By the time she opens her eyes and tries to move she feels a sharp pain in her left arm. It was only seconds, but as she turns her head to see what happened, she sees Tara standing there pulling a needle out of her arm. Mitch jumps up. "What the fuck are you doing Tara?" Mitch yells out. Tara just stands there looking at Mitch and blows her a kiss with a smile, Mitch tries to reach out to grab Tara but the drug is already taking affect on her, Mitch drops to her knees. Tara tells Mitch to count backwards from ten and then starts to laugh, that's the last thing Mitch hears before she is out cold and falls from her knees to the floor face down. Cindy jumps up from her chair and begs for her life to Tara. Tara tells her to relax." I'm not going to kill you, but you are going to help me with this bullshit now."

Tara goes and grabs two sets of handcuffs and places them on Mitch, one set on her wrists and the other set on her ankles, they are tight on her ankles and digging into her skin a bit but she just wants to make sure Mitch can't do anything if she wakes up too soon. Cindy is not sure what to think of what is going on. Mitch told her she would set her free if she listened to her, now Tara is drugging her and cuffing her on the ground. Cindy starts to shake with apprehension and some fear that Tara will kill her. She said she wouldn't but how the hell can she trust any of these mentally unstable bunch of fucks she has been thrown together with.

Tara looks over at Cindy and tells her to stop just standing there and help her try to fix this woman up. Tara goes and gets some sutures to try and close the open gapping-bloody hole in her chest and side. Tara comes back and sits down and gets out some lidocain and shoots it into the areas around the hole. Then she takes a pair of needle nose pliers and grabs the small needle attached to the suture. The needle nose pliers are not the proper tool to use but Tara is no doctor so it doesn't really matter at this point, she just wants to try and close her up to see if she can keep her alive for awhile. Keep her for Mitch maybe when she fully decides what she is going to do with Mitch.

Mitch was always the one who thought she could play Doctor God with people. Tara and Christa only tortured and hacked women up just for the thrill of it. Mitch always had wanted more, wanted everything from them.

Cindy asks Tara why she is trying to help this woman and not kill her. Tara just says she has her reasons now and not to worry about why she is doing what she is doing. Tara is reaching in the cavity with the needle and trying to sew up the layers on the way out, she has no idea what she is doing though. Tara does the best she can layer by layer until she reaches the skin and stitches it up half ass, but the lady is still alive, at least for now. Tara looks at the woman she has just crudely sewn up and sees tears running down her face and her eyes are shut tight. Tara takes the towel out of her mouth now and gives her a few sips of water so she isn't so dry. Tara grabs some pain medicine, morphine, and shoots it into the IV to help her with the pain. Tara lets her know as she lies there in the most unthinkable pain she has ever felt in her life, that she is missing ribs on the left side and she did the best should could to sew her up. Tara also let her know she can have as much pain medicine as she wants. The woman on the table tells her to please just let her go, drive her somewhere and just leave her, that someone will find her and help her. That she will never say a word, she could barely muster out of her dry throat. Tara just tells her that's not possible right now and to just hang in there as she has more pressing issues right now. They just leave her strapped to the table with the IV slowly dripping the morphine into her veins without another thought about her for now.

Chapter 26

Tara tells Cindy in a stern voice to help her to move Mitch to the chair with the restraints on it that is sitting in the corner of the room. They both put one arm under Mitch's arms and move her over to the chair with her boots dragging behind her limp body across the smooth cement floor. Once they have her in the old wooden chair they begin to strap her arms and legs to the chair, and place one extra strap around her chest to hold her tight incase she wakes up sooner than later on them. They lock the restraints with the key and Tara places the key in her front pocket of her ripped up blue jeans. Tara grabs the small stool and sits down and just stares at Mitch sitting limp in the chair. Her eyes closed with mouth slightly opened. She looks so peaceful as she slumbers. Tara knows once Mitch wakes up she is going to be fucking pissed off to no end. She just stares at Mitch with her head in her hand rubbing her forehead searching for her next step.

It's so quite you can hear the clock on the wall ticking second by second. The sound was broken by Cindy's voice. Tara could hear her talking but was just so tuned out to it trying to think. Tara's eyes slowly move up to Cindy's face and she can start to hear her more clearly as she comes back to reality, Cindy keeps saying, " She's not breathing, she's not breathing!" Cindy just points to the woman on the table as she is trying to tell Tara that the woman is not breathing and what should they do. Tara gets up off the stool and walks over to the woman strapped to the table and checks for a pulse with their backs turned toward Mitch. Mitch starts to awaken and is so groggy she can't even focus on one part of the room or on the people in the room. Tara starts telling Cindy that the woman is dead and there is nothing she can do now, as the words are coming out of Tara's mouth she turns around and sees that Mitch is waking up from her drugged slumber. Mitch moans and mumbles some words they can't make out as her head bobs down a few times as she tries to get her wits about her and focus. Cindy starts to freak out and rushes over to un-strap Mitch from the restraints, Tara grabs Cindy and pulls her back away from Mitch.

"What the hell do you think you're doing? Leave her tied down or I'll lock you back up in your little room in the dark to die all alone." Tara tells Cindy. Cindy looks at Tara and says, "Please I don't want to make her mad, she will kill me for sure, please Tara."

Tara tells Cindy to just calm down and take a breath, nothing is happening. "Mitch isn't going to kill anyone while she is tied up. So you can stay in here and be quite or you can go back into the room to wait with the door locked to die. Either way, just let me know now, either sit down or be locked up." Cindy walks slowly and quietly over to another stool in the room on the other side of table where the woman lies dead and still. Tara pulls up the stool and sits down in front of Mitch. Mitch is looking at Tara and asks what is going on, why has she tied her down and drugged her. Mitch remains calm as she looks Tara in the eyes and waits for an answer.

Tara isn't sure what to really say or where to start to explain. Tara knows at this point she is kind of fucked because Mitch will surely hurt her now, or worse. Love isn't enough to undo being drugged and strapped down to your own torture chair, is it? Tara starts to tell Mitch that she can't believe she is fucking someone else after they had agreed to make a go out of a relationship between them. That she is hurt that she would give herself to another woman when Tara has loved her for so long, given her blood and pain too. Tara brings up Christa and how could she just throw her away so quickly, after all, Christa had been a friend to Mitch much longer than Tara and just like that she killed her to save herself. “You said it was for us.” Tara continues on. “But was it? Or was it so you wouldn’t get caught and go to prison, you, not for us. I bet if I did something you would discard me too wouldn’t you Mitch!” There is silence for a moment. Then Tara asks. “Mitch, what did Christa mean when she said to me, Mitch and I took you when you were younger? What did she mean Mitch? Tell me now! You say you love me but all you do is fucking lie and fuck other women Mitch!” Tara yells at Mitch then just waits for answers.

Mitch is a bit surprised by Tara speaking her mind to her that way, but Mitch just smiles and puts her head down for a moment. Tara sees her smiling and asks her what's so damn funny! Mitch lifts her head up and looks at Tara, still with a big smile on her face. "We need to talk but not like this, we need to talk alone and you really need to untie me. Let's just go somewhere alone and talk Tara." Tara just shakes her head no and stands up quickly and tells Cindy to come with her now, Tara is getting more and more upset because Mitch just sits there and smiles when she is trying to be serious and get some answers. Answers to this mess that has become their lives ever since Christa was killed for just trying to please Mitch. Mitch cheating on her when they have just begun to be together after all these years. The anger just builds in Tara. Tara takes Cindy into the other room where she is being kept and locks her in there. Tara tells her she just needs to talk to Mitch alone and she will be back soon.

Before Tara walks out of the room, she asks Cindy about yesterday, “What did you and Mitch talk about in her yesterday?” Cindy doesn’t know how to answer. Tara looks at her and tells her, “If you lie to me I will slowly cut you apart limb by fucking limb, so be very honest with me.” Cindy answers slowly, “We just talked and Mitch kissed me a little, she just told me she wanted to teach me. She said she wanted to fuck me. She just kissed my neck and lips a little. That’s all that happened, nothing did happen Tara!” Cindy doesn’t say anything more as the door closes and she hears the bolt turn and lock on the door. Tears just roll down her face as she drops to the ground, distraught with fear, and just cry's out loudly. She is worried that she will be tortured and killed for sure now and that Mitch will be so pissed at her for helping to tie her down to that chair and not helping her. She is beside herself in this hell she knows now and there is just no way out of. Cindy just lies on the floor crying and praying for God to take her quickly, she has no hope of ever getting out alive ever again, to never see the light of day or her family and friends. To never feel joy or happiness, now her only life will be as a slave or to be murdered in a horrible way she can't wrap her head around. Mitch at least gave her some kind of hope and was very nice and understanding with her, she had felt hope, ever slight, but hope with Mitch. She doesn't have that with Tara, she feels Tara doesn't want her there and will just get rid of her as soon as she can. Cindy also wonders why would Tara drugged and tied up Mitch. What had happened so badly to make this happen or are they so damn insane they don't even realize what is happening in their little world they have built around them.

Tara walks back into the room with Mitch and sits down in front of her, she tells Mitch that she is ready to talk it out, that she loves her but needs to understand why she has slept with this other woman and why was it so easy to just dispose of Christa. Mitch asks for some water, as she is dry from being drugged. Tara gives her a few big sips from a bottle of water and waits to hear what Mitch has to say. She is angry sitting there with her arms and legs crossed tightly with her jaw clinching together. Tara is trying not to show how angry she is but she just can't seem to help it and doesn't realize how much anger she is actually showing to Mitch.

Mitch clears her throat and begins to apologize to Tara for her fucking that woman from work. She tries to explain it was only twice and it meant nothing to her, just sex, nothing more and nothing less to her. Mitch goes on to tell her how much she loves her and never meant to hurt her. Mitch goes on and on about it, trying to make Tara see it was nothing. She also tells her about Christa and how she did it for them, for Tara. How she would do anything to protect her from ever being taken away or hurt. How Christa put them all in jeopardy and it was the right thing to do to protect them all. Mitch asks Tara if she would rather go to prison for the rest of her life of or just get rid of one person. Mitch can tell she is making no headway with Tara at all, that Tara just sits there getting more and angrier. Her anger shows in her eyes, as Mitch looks deep into them. Mitch is trying to now sweet talk her way out of being strapped down to the chair, she hates being unable to move, the feeling of being helpless. Now she knows how it feels for the women they have taken over the years, she wants to just scream and yell at Tara to untie her now. Mitch knows she can’t do it that way or she will never untie her. Mitch stops talking and just looks at Tara, she’s trying to look sad and pathetic so Tara will hopefully feel bad and just let her free at this point. It’s been over an hour and still she is bound to this chair, Mitch knows she has to do something to get out of this.

Tara jumps up off the stool and tells Mitch she needs a break, she just need to think for a bit. Tara starts to walk out of the room and shut the door to enclose Mitch even more. Mitch yells to Tara, “Hey, you’re not going to just leave me in here tied up are you? I have to take a piss let me up now!” Tara doesn’t even look at her and just shuts and locks the door and goes upstairs. Mitch starts yelling and screaming as loud as she can to come back and set her free, that if she doesn’t she will kill her. After what seems like forever Mitch finally stops screaming and trying to break out of her straps from the chair, it has wore her down and she sits there all sweaty and her throat is getting sore. Mitch can’t believe she just left her there, locked away like she was nothing. Mitch just tries to calm herself down and think about how to get to Tara, to bring her back to her.

Chapter 27

Tara is sitting at the kitchen table and sees Mitch's cell phone sitting there, she picks up the phone and starts looking through her text messages and numbers list. As she is looking through her phone she doesn't see anything strange or any conversations with any women.

Everything seems either work related or to Tara, she even sees some old text messages to Christa still on there as well. She takes a big breath and thinks maybe she has been too hasty with Mitch. Maybe Mitch was just afraid of making a new relationship with her and fucked that woman out of fear. She thinks if there was something real between them there would be some kind of messages between the two of them, wouldn't there? She also ponders the messages from Christa and how close they truly were. It must have been hard for Mitch to kill her and take away the long friendship that they had. Tara puts her head in her hands and just tries to sort it out in her mind, and even wonders if she is being overbearing or just too damn jealous or insecure about everything. Maybe it has something to do with Mitch wanting to keep the other girl around and train her to become a murderer; she's just not sure what to think at this point. Tara gets up and goes outside for some air before going back to see Mitch. She has calmed down and maybe she needs to just let Mitch know how much she really means to her, before un-strapping her of course.

Back downstairs Mitch is thinking that she needs to just come totally clean with Tara and tell her everything. Mitch is also wondering why Tara is being so crazy and maybe it does have something to do with her wanting to keep the woman around to become like them. Maybe it is making her remember something, the something they have been keeping from her for a long time. Mitch is just so unsure if she should tell Tara everything, about Christa, about them and how they really became this crazy group of people that found them selves together and living this life that they do. Mitch thinks this is the only way and she will tell Tara when she comes back downstairs to see her, she hopes she hasn't remembered anything yet and just took off to let her rot away to die. Mitch laughs as she sits there and thinks about what she had always been told, never lie because you always get caught in a web. Now she is in her own web like prey waiting to be eaten up by a black spider she made in her own lab. Mitch just keeps laughing thinking how fucked this has all become, her kingdom on the verge of collapse. Mitch thinks too it might be a good idea to torture the woman and not keep her, maybe that would make Tara feel more secure and that there is no misunderstanding about why she wants to keep her around. Mitch just can't help think maybe

Tara has or is remembering something. Mitch hears a noise, it's the door to their secret basement and Tara must be coming back down to talk to her.

The door opens slowly and Tara appears and walks through the doorway into the room where Mitch is sitting. Before Tara can even say a word, Mitch tells her to sit down and just listen, she wants to tell her everything. Tara sits down on the stool in front of Mitch. Mitch looks at her and noticed how sexy Tara is, she's wearing a white tank top and ripped up worn out blue jeans and her hair and makeup just look so perfect. Her piercings in her face make her look so bad ass hot, Mitch thinks. Mitch takes a deep breath in and begins to tell Tara everything.

Mitch starts to explain, "Tara, what I'm going to tell you might not matter but I think I need to tell you everything. Then you will understand me and us better. In fact, I think it will bring us even closer together. Christa and I had been friends forever, a very long time, and years before I ever saw you. We grew up close to each other and even though she is much younger then me, we became fast friends and even liked the same things. Like watching girls, talking about them and then we started hunting them, as we called it. Then before we knew it we were taking them, hiding them and killing them. That's why I bought this farmhouse, far away from anyone else. Yes, she was weird and different and liked smoking weed but for some reason it just worked. It worked for five or so years, then one day we were out fishing and camping. It was a couple hours from here, and I saw you walking down a trail. I was coming up from the lake and I saw you, you took my breath away, as I walked past you I got butterflies in my stomach, a feeling I had never felt before. You were so young, so pretty and innocent. I just knew you needed to be with me, to be a part of us. I went and told Christa about you and we came back up the trail and followed you to a cabin you were staying at with your family."

Tara interrupts Mitch in a confused but upset tone, "I'm sorry, what are you saying? I don't remember my family. I don't remember anything you're fucking telling me. What does this have to do with anything?"

"Shhh, just listen Tara. Long story short then, Christa and I took you. You went out late one evening from the cabin and we took you with us. We brought you back here and you became one of us, you became a friend and our family. That's what Christa was trying to tell you, but thank God you stuck that towel in her mouth to shut her up. You are one of us Tara. Just like us. A killer, murderer, and a fucking monster like us. I made you."

Tara stands up and starts yelling at Mitch, she doesn't remember anything like that. "What does that mean you took me? You took me as in I fell for you or you two took me as in what!" Tara screamed for answers and fast, she was getting more and more upset. Mitch tells Tara to untie her and she can show her exactly what she means, showing is better then trying to explain it maybe.

Tara storms out of the room and goes into the hallway shutting the door behind her. Tara leans up against the wall and thinks back to her childhood, nothing is coming to her mind, why can't she remember her family, or any camping trip at a cabin. She doesn't remember holidays, birthdays or even going to school. Tara for the life of her doesn't understand why she has never even thought about these things or wondered about them before now. Tara thinks maybe she was in an accident or something. Maybe she lost her memory. Tara tries so hard to remember anything but can only remember back a few years or so and all the memories are of Mitch, Christa, this house and her job at the bar. "That's it!" Tara exclaimed out loud. I'm ok. Everything is ok. Whew! And if they had taken me away from my family I wouldn't be able to be let out to come and go as I please and to have a job. Tara starts to laugh with relief and knows it must have been some kind of accident and maybe her family was killed and Mitch has taken care of her all these years. That must be it she thinks. Tara collects herself and walks back into the room with Mitch and tells Mitch to finish telling her.

Mitch asks Tara again, "Just un-strap me and I'll show you what happened." Mitch tells Tara how much she loves her and wants to start again. Tara does want to know what Mitch has to show her so she tells Mitch to just tell her where to look, where can she find this information at and she will go look for herself. Mitch doesn't want to do that but she thinks this might be the only way that Tara will un-strap her from the chair. So Mitch tells Tara to go up into her bedroom and under the bed there is a small trap door and to open it, inside she will find flyers and other paperwork in there about everything and everyone. But you have to promise to come back down here after you look and before you do anything else. Tara asks her why she wouldn't come back down afterward. 'What the fuck is going on Mitch." Mitch just tells her to go and look and make sure to come back. Tara leaves the room but leaves the door open this time to where Mitch is. Mitch hopes this is the right thing to do, either way she thinks Tara will come back and un-strap her from this damn chair. Either she will be really excited or really fucking pissed but either way she should want Mitch up and out of this chair.

Chapter 28

Tara is at the bottom of the stairway and looks up to Mitch's bedroom door, she freezes a moment and is somewhat worried about what she will find up there. What could be the big deal, after all they share and know everything about each other, and they have killed together.

What could Mitch have that would make a difference to anything? Tara walks up the stairs and into the bedroom and kneels down to look under the bed. She does see a small area that looks like a false floor. She tries to open it but there is no way to just open it up. She goes and gets a screw driver and puts the end in a small slit and pops it open, she can't see anything as it is too far back so she just reaches in to pull out all this paperwork. She gets everything out of there and leaves the little hole empty and takes the paperwork and goes through it page by page, not seeing anything strange. The paperwork consists of flyer after flyer with missing girls and women on them. It shows their picture, name, age, and location they went missing and has a phone number to call if you have seen them. Some of the girls she doesn't recognize but some she does from when they had taken those women. Tara has a perplexed look on her face when she gets to one of the flyers, the girl looks so familiar but she just can't place her. The girl in the picture has short hair and went missing at the age of twelve. Tara can't take her eyes off this flyer. She gets up and goes over to the mirror and looks at herself and then holds the flyer up next to her reflection. She just keeps looking at herself then at the flyer and then it hits her like a ton of bricks. "It's me." Tara whispers. Tara can't believe it. It is her on that flyer, but how can this be. She almost becomes numb and can't fathom how this could be. I'm a missing girl she wonders. She takes the flyer and rushes downstairs to the computer in the living room and looks up the name on the flyer. The name on the flyer is Tammy Whitman age twelve. She puts it into the computer search and waits. Within a few seconds the screen is flooded with information about this girl and her family. It says Tammy Whitman age twelve went missing from a state park in Washington State and her family is searching for her. The article went on to say even though her family went back to Phoenix, AZ they haven't given up on the search and won't give up until she is found. The date on this article was from ten years ago. Tara sits there in shock. Is that the park that Mitch spoke of? And there was no accident like she had thought? And her name, Tara Biltmore, is not real? Her name is Tammy Whitman?

Tara gets up and walks outside with the flyer in hand and just looks up at the sky and wonders is this a joke, is this true? Was she an innocent girl once who is now a monster? She walks into the field and lays there awhile just staring up at the sky, watching the clouds trying to take this all in. As she lays there she wonders, how can I go to work and no one knows, why haven't I ran away? What is this place? Who am I really? I have a family? All these things she wonders as she's just in a kind of trance looking at the beautiful sky above her. After awhile she gets up and looks at the house, she knows she needs to confront Mitch, she's just not sure how to feel. She only knows she feels hurt and betrayed at this moment. Everything is a lie. What does she do now? She only knows this place, this life. She doesn't remember anything else. Is she a true monster, taking women for her own pleasure? Would I be in trouble for killing or would I be ok? Am I a victim? She just isn't sure where to start, what to do with this information and why would Mitch tell her now. She walks back in the only home she knows and just sits in the living room to think and process what this all really means.

After some time of thinking Tara gets back on the computer and looks up more about herself. She sees pictures of her mother and father and that every few years they do interviews about their missing daughter and try to help other families cope with this same issue. She can't believe she's from Phoenix, AZ either, she doesn't know it.

She now sees Mitch as a monster in the basement. She has had sex with her. She's in love with her, that's the hardest part for Tara to except, that she really is in love with her. Tara goes to the mirror that's placed above the mantel in the living room and looks at herself. She asks herself what to do now.

Chapter 29

Mitch is struggling to escape from the chair but knows she won't get out. She has made everything so women couldn't just wiggle their way out to freedom. She looks at the clock on the wall and noticed Tara left her hours ago and can't believe she hasn't been back down to check on her or anything. Just then she hears the door to the basement open and close and can hear Tara walking toward the room, Mitch sits up and waits for Tara to walk into the room. Tara just peeks in at Mitch and then shuts the door. Mitch can't believe it. Mitch hears Tara go over to one of the rooms down the hallway and opens it, she can her talking but can't make out what they are saying. She knows Tara will come in any moment so she tries to wait and look happy for when she comes in there to see her.

Tara has gone into the room where Mitch's pet is, Cindy. Tara has the flyer in hand and hands it to Cindy to look at. Cindy takes a look at it and asks Tara who is the girl in the picture? Tara tells her to look at it and then look at her. "It's me! Mitch has taken me away from my family, just like she took you from yours."

Cindy looks at the picture and then back at Tara several times before she then also sees that it is in fact Tara in the picture on the flyer. Cindy's eyes tear up and she looks at Tara and asks, "When did you know, when did you find out about this?" Tara tells her that she just found out a few hours ago and she still can't believe it. Cindy asks her why she is telling her. "What happens now, can we leave and call the police? Yes! We must call the police and leave." Just then Cindy gets a big smile on her face and starts to laugh with joy and gets up to her feet and stands before Tara. She just keeps telling Tara to call the police and for them to leave now. Tara shakes her head no, and puts her hand and arm out with palm facing Cindy. She tells her they are not going to do anything yet, and that she is not sure how to handle this now, everything has changed. She also tells Cindy she just wanted her to know that she was not always a monster, “I used to be normal like you but I don’t remember those times, now I’m just normal as we are now.” Tara lets her know she is going to shut the door and lock her back in for awhile until she can figure this all out in her head and what should be done next. Cindy gets a horrified look on her face and yells at Tara, “NO, NO, we need to go now, what the fuck is wrong with you!” Then she lunges at Tara and for the door to run out but doesn’t get far. Tara holds her back and shoves her to the floor and then leaves the room quickly, slamming and locking the door behind her. Cindy goes to the door and is screaming and pounding on the door for her to come back, to just please come back and save them both.

Tara then walks to the door where Mitch is and opens it and walks in and shows her the flyer. Mitch smiles at her and says, "I love you. I always have and always will love you Tara. That's why you're here with me now." Tara closes the door behind her and asks Mitch why she can't remember the life she took her away from then if this is true. She then asks if this flyer is real, or is it just a mind fuck of some kind. Tara waits for Mitch to answer.

Mitch starts to again explain to her but starts from where she left off before. "After we took you, we kept you in the last room where Cindy is now, we kept you in the dark, all alone. We never spoke to you or touched you. We only brought you food and water for three years. That was the hardest part for me, to pretend like you where not even here in this house with us, I wanted you for so long. Christa came in there the most so I didn't have to, I just felt I couldn't, that I would have been too tempted to touch you or talk to you." As Mitch speaks and tells Tara, tears just roll down Tara's face, she tries to control it but the tears just flow. "We would leave you letters we wrote in there from time to time that said they were from your parents and how they hated you and they were so glad that you were gone from their lives. That's the only time we would leave the lights on in there, for an hour or so. Christa and I would take turns raping you with objects then just leave you in the dark again, fuck you and just leave you. We would do this over the years. Then we both started talking to you. You wanted to just hear someone's voice so badly. If you were good and listened to us we would talk to you and leave the lights on, but if you wanted to act out we left you for days at a time without food, water or human contact after that. Another year went by and then I started going in the room with you, holding you, and telling you how much I loved you and glad that you are here with us. I started having sex with you, gently, kindly. I made love to you, talked to you sweetly. All the while still giving you letters from your family about how much they hated you. Then slowly bringing you out to the other rooms little by little then strapping you down to this very table and giving you small electrical shocks to your forehead, the front of your brain. I thought we were going to lose you a few times, but you made it through all of it. You were confused a lot of the time after the shocks but we took our time with you and slowly brought you upstairs to live with us. I made you Tara. I made you love me. Every time you would talk about your past we would just tell you were crazy, that this was just made up in your head and then we would give you a few more small shocks. When you asked about pictures of you growing up, we told you there was a fire and everything was destroyed. You were my first to ever try that on, my love. You're everything to me. I never hurt you. I never let Christa hurt you. Then we slowly introduced you to killing, raping and taking women. It was a long process over six years but here you are now, another five years after that. Now you love me like I always hoped you would, and you kill like me. You take pleasure in it knowing it makes me happy. So that's it, that's how you become part of us. You're my sexy little killer. Don't forget, I killed my best friend for you Tara, I killed Christa, for you!"

Tara is just beside herself sitting on the stool just looking at Mitch, looking her right in the face and can't believe this is real. "You fucking took my life away from me, you brainwashed me Mitch!" Tara says loudly as she fights back tears as she continues to say, "I thought you were just cheating on me and I was going to teach you a lesson and show you how much I love you, but you are a fucking piece of shit Mitch. No wonder I don't see people as human like us, I see them as stupid living masses, because of you."

"What are you going to do now? You belong here now, you think you can just walk out of here and the humans that live out there in the world wouldn't lock you away? You need me Tara. We need each other now more than ever. Come on, un-strap me from this chair and let me hold you now. You need to just cry, scream and even hit me I'm sure. But it's been too long. You have kidnapped and killed too many women over the years. Not only have you killed them, you tore them apart with me. You are a savage beast. They will never understand Tara. Come on, let me help you now my love". Mitch says to Tara trying to be released from that chair. As she spoke to Tara she did it was such kindness and love, shoving down her anger, as Mitch only wants to be free now.

Tara just looks at her with confusion. "Ok if this is true, how can I have a job at the bar and work outside and have freedom? You wouldn't let me out of your sight in fear of me running away or telling someone about what you did to me!" Tara yells.

"I saw him one night a long time ago, let's just say he was doing something not so nice to a girl in the back of that bar one night. So I held that over his head for a long time, but sometimes I would take girls and give them to him. I never asked what he did to them nor do I care either. I just told him to watch you while you were there working and if you ever started acting strange to take you and hold you quietly until I got there. But it never came to that, you just went to work and never thought anything of it. He was always nice to right? There is a reason. He doesn't want to go to prison anymore than I do. That's how I know you love me, you've always loved me, you always came home, and you cooked and cleaned for me. You just never remembered anything to know any different, just like you don't remember anything now, I don't think you ever will." Mitch said to Tara.

Tara looks at Mitch and tells her she asked Cindy what they talked about the day before. Tara tells Mitch that Cindy told on her, told her everything. "So you want to fuck Cindy now too, teach her too? You are so fucked Mitch! I love you, God this is so fucked!" Tara screams at Mitch. Mitch tries not to smile but she can't help herself, she is getting off on Tara being so upset.

Chapter 30

Tara sits upstairs in Mitch's room on her bed. She feels the soft sheets on her hands and can't believe she has made love to her right here on this bed. She leans down and smells the pillow. It smells just like Mitch with the combination of her perfume and shampoo trapped in the pillow. She is so angered but yet so very confused on what to do, she really does have feelings of love for Mitch. She just doesn't know if these are real feelings or just brainwashed lies. Is she now going to be replaced by Cindy and then just thrown away like Christa? Is she a victim or would she be in trouble for taking and killing dozens of women over the years with Mitch? How could she not remember being kidnapped herself? Tara just sits there with all these questions running through her head and she just doesn't know what to do. Does she go to the police, run away or stay? She just doesn't know what to do or think. She breaks down in tears on the bed and just sobs uncontrollably all alone.

Tara has cried until she has no more tears to cry, nothing left. She gets up off the bed and takes a much needed shower and just lets the water rush over her face and body. She uses Mitch's soap and shampoo to smell her again, to be close to her. She gets out of the shower and takes her time getting ready, putting on her makeup and doing her hair straight and flowing just the way Mitch likes it. She puts on another pair of torn worn out blue jeans and a tight fitting tank top with her black ankle high boots. She looks in the mirror and says, "Tara your looking hot bitch!" Then she laughs and checks her piercings to make sure they are all in tight.

Tara goes downstairs and gets Cindy out of the room she is being kept in and tells her to follow her into the room where Mitch is. Tara is being very nice to Cindy. Cindy does as she is asked and is hoping that Tara has come to her senses and is going to call the police and this will be all over. As soon as Cindy enters the room Tara pulls out her gun and points it at Cindy's head. Tara tells her to move the other chair and place it right in front of Mitch. Mitch smiles as soon as she sees Tara and tells her how beautiful she is. Tara smiles back at Mitch while pointing and instructing Cindy on what to do. "Now sit down in the chair Cindy and shut up or I'll fucking shoot you. I won't kill you but I will shoot you." Cindy sits down reluctantly in the chair and Tara takes duct tape and tapes her hands and wrists to the arms of the chair. Then tapes her ankles to the front legs of the chair. "There we go, now we are all together. Mitch you are facing your new little fucking pet and Cindy, well you're just fucked because Mitch wants you." Tara tells them as she stands and looks over both of them. Cindy starts to yell,

"Just call the police Tara, stop this now, call the police what the fuck are you waiting for? Help us!" Tara strikes Cindy in the face with her gun and yells at her to shut the fuck up. Tara doesn't want to hear from her anymore so she shoves a dirty towel in her mouth and duct tapes it in place, wrapping tape around her head and over her mouth three to four times.

"Ok now that she is quite, Oh Mitch, I do love you so very much. But then you know that already, you made me, you made me love you. We have made love. You created me with nothing but your love." Tara says to Mitch in a soft caring voice. Mitch smiles and tells her yes, it was all done with love for her. Tara walks behind Mitch and kisses her neck and starts to rub her shoulder with one hand and then with the other hand she shoves a towel deep in her mouth.

Mitch's eyes open wide and can't believe that Tara just shoved a towel in her mouth. Mitch starts to gag on the towel and uses her tongue to try and shove it out but she can't move it at all. Tara then grabs a piece of tape and rips a small piece and places it over her mouth "There we go, now you can just be fucking quite for awhile Mitch." Tara says with a smile while close in toward Mitch's face.

"Well I guess I have the floor now. Cindy I do want to tell you that yes, Mitch was really going to let you go free after she had her fun with you and tried to make you a monster. The only difference is she wasn't going to just let you walk out of here just like that. She told me she was going to stab you in your ears so you could not hear, busting your eardrums. Then she was going to gorge out your eyes from your head so you could not see, then cut your tongue out so you would never speak again. Then ending with cutting both your hands clear off your body. That's what you begged her for. You still want me to let her go?" Tara asked Cindy.

Cindy shook her head no quickly as tears rolled down her face. Mitch just sits there shaking her head while trying to breath through her nose. Mitch doesn't know what to expect at this point but doesn't expect much from Tara. She just hopes Tara will get her anger out and set her free, so she tries to remain calm. But she can't help feeling helpless and hopeless, as there is not one thing she can do or say, being tied up and not being able to speak is the worst thing she has ever felt in her life. Mitch wishes Christa was here now to help her from this, but Mitch's heart fills full of sorrow knowing she took

Christa away from herself. Mitch all the sudden snaps out of it and believes that Tara does love her and will set her free soon. Mitch brightens up and just takes Tara's yelling and nonsense.

"You know I have a lot of anger right now, rage built up inside me, thank you Mitch." Tara says as she walks over and picks up a hammer off the counter and walks over to Mitch and without another thought she swings the hammer down hitting Mitch's right knee hard. You can hear the loud crack of her kneecap. Mitch tries to scream out and rises up from the chair as much as she can in pain. Mitch starts scrambling to get off the chair to get away but as she tries to escape, Tara raises the hammer again and with all her might slams is down on Mitch's left knee. Another loud snapping and cracking, the cuffs are cutting into Mitch's ankles as she tries to pull away from the chair, just digging into her flesh. The pain is unbearable and Mitch tries to scream for Tara to stop but not much comes out, just muffled sounds, like all the women she has taken. "I'm sorry, are you trying to tell me something Mitch? I can't hear you, speak up." Tara asks Mitch while she starts to laugh. Tara tells her, "Now you know how it feels to be taking apart little by little, piece by piece." The more Tara looks at Mitch and thinks about all the lies she has told her the more enraged she becomes. Tara takes the hammer to Mitch and starts hammering away on her arms and her legs just smashing them to bits one swing at a time. There's nothing that Mitch can do but just take swing after painful swing. Mitch is crying and screaming muffled through the towel with tears rushing down her face as she tries to find a way out of this now. Her hell is now what she has created. Taken down by her own human creature she has made over the years. She thought for sure telling Tara the truth would set her free.

Tara stands there looking at Mitch, never seeing her like this before, in this horrible state of fear and sadness and pain. Tara feels good, really good. Tara leans down to Mitch and kisses her face and tells her the pain is over, “It’s over my love.” Tara un-straps Mitch from the chair, but now Mitch cannot move on her own, her arms and legs are just broken and busted. Tara grabs Mitch by the legs and pulls her out of the chair, her back and head hitting the cement floor hard, making her a little dizzy but not knocking her out. Cindy looks on and can’t believe what she is seeing, not sure if she should feel relief or be even more afraid as she watches Tara drag Mitch out of the room, blood trailing behind her. Cindy is in a slight state of shock not being able to comprehend this right now.

Tara drags Mitch out of the room and down the hallway to the other set of steps to the dirt holes, she swings the door open and gets Mitch as close as she can and pushes her down the stairs. Mitch's body just falls freely down the stairs hitting the bottom kicking up dust as her body settles on the dirt floor. Mitch can't move and is now in total darkness and in the worst pain she has ever felt. Tara flips on the light for a second to make sure Mitch isn't face down in the dirt and is able to still breathe. "Oh sweetie you're ok, I'll be down in moment." Tara sweetly yells down to Mitch. Mitch is just left there to moan and groan in pain. She tries to move, but she is just so broken, and hurt.

Tara goes back upstairs to Cindy, "This is your lucky day! You get to go free but you have to help me first, ok?" Cindy shakes her head yes and is just so happy that Tara looks so friendly and tells her she will let her go. Cindy has no reason to doubt this at this point because she feels they are the same, both victims of being stolen away and abused. Tara cuts the tape and apologizes to Cindy for taping her to the chair; she explains she just didn't want her to stop her from doing what she had to do to Mitch. Cindy says she doesn't care as long as they are getting the hell out of there. Tara has Cindy go first down the stairs and tells her she needs to bury the body. Cindy stops and turns and asks why. "We need to just call the police Tara!" Cindy says with excitement in her voice. Tara lets Cindy know she doesn't want Mitch to live in a jail or in some mental institution, she doesn't want her to suffer that much, she still loves her. Tara asks if she is with her or not, before Cindy could answer Tara shoots her in the leg and Cindy drops down losing the leg from under her and falls straight to the bottom missing the rest of the stairs on the way down, landing half way on Mitch and the other half in the lose dusty dirt. Cindy is screaming out in pain and cussing at Tara.

Tara flips on the lights and slowly walks down the stairs to where they both lie in pain. Tara takes the towel out of Mitch's mouth and shoves it in Cindy's mouth so she doesn't have to hear her screaming any more. "God shut the fuck up already! I have no idea what Mitch sees in you!" Tara yelled right in her face. Tara picks up a shovel and starts digging a hole, as she digs Mitch calls out to her in a whisper, "Tara please help me, I'm sorry. I truly do love you, help me Tara." Tara lets Mitch know she loves her too and says no more and just keeps digging. After almost an hour of digging, she walks over to Cindy and shoots her in both her arms at the elbow. Cindy screams as loud as she can in pain and just starts to flail around on the dirt floor, but the screams are only heard quietly as they are muffled by the wet nasty towel placed in her mouth from Mitch's. Tara grabs Cindy's ankles and drags her over to the shallow hole and pushes her down in the dark hole with her foot. Tara takes the shovel and puts a few shovels full of dirt on top of her. All the while Cindy tries to scream out. Tara throws down the shovel and walks over to Mitch and lies on the dirt floor next to her.

Tara is stroking Mitch's hair softly and tells her she loves her very much as tears roll down Tara's face. "The funny part is, I was only going to teach you a lesson for cheating, but I'm glad you showed me the light Mitch." Mitch responded, "I just wanted to be honest with you because I love you so much. I thought you would see I did it for you Tara." Tara just laughs softly and kisses her on her forehead. She whispers to Mitch, that she will never forget her. Then drags her over to the hole where Cindy is. She give Mitch one last long kiss and then kicks her body on top of Cindy's body, you just hear moans and coughs as Tara places dirt on top of both of them. "Now you'll never be alone Mitch, you will be with all your girls forever." Tara keeps shoveling dirt until the hole is gone and no more moans or groans can be heard. She leans down and pats the dirt a few times then walks upstairs turning the lights off. Tara opens the door and one woman remains. Tara just shoots her in the head and walks out. No more sounds, no more people in the house but Tara. Everything is quite as Tara leaves the basement and heads upstairs.

Chapter 31

Tara fixes herself a drink and goes and sits on the front porch for a while, looking out on all the beauty, the flowers blowing in the wind, the sun hitting her face feels so nice. Everything just looks and feels better to Tara. She's not sure why but it just does.

Tara walks inside and picks up Mitch's cell phone, she finds the number for her boss at the bar that Mitch knew that gave her the job there. She text him as Mitch and says Tara is gone. Plain and simple, so that he won't expect her back or try and come out to the farmhouse looking for Tara or Mitch. Tara knows she only has a few days before Mitch is suppose to be back at work.

Tara packs a small bag and goes into Mitch's room and pulls back the desk away from the wall, there is a hidden door she has seen Mitch keep things in. She finds some documents for the house, jewelry, a few handguns and some money. Tara only takes the cash. It's not much but it's enough for her to get somewhere, to start again maybe.

Tara grabs her small bag and walks out to her car, gets in and doesn't look back. She looks at the flyer and some paperwork she took with the address to her parent's house and drives away. Tara looks into the rearview window and says, "Damn bitch you are looking good!" She turns on the radio and just drives. Tara isn't sure if she will ever go home, to a home she never knew, she has nothing now and no one. She thinks she will just see what she can do and hopes she can be a better person. But after a few weeks, will she start falling back into old habits? Watching women on the road as she travels? Following them without approaching them? She misses Mitch more than she thought. It makes her feel empty inside. She needed her in a weird way.

Chapter 32

While just driving around Tara sees a sign that says Phoenix route 17, Tara takes it and drives toward Phoenix where she is from. She doesn’t remember it at all and as she drives and enters into the city limits nothing she sees reminds her of her past or childhood. The only past she can remember is with Christa and Mitch. She looks at a map and finds her parents home, not sure if they even live there anymore.

Tara camps out by her parent's house for two weeks, watching their movements, what their schedules are, to learn when they come and go. She does know it's them from searching the web and seeing their pictures. Two weeks have gone by and she waits, but on this day the wait is over, it's a Friday. They both leave going to work. As she sits in her car, she places a blonde wig on her head and big sunglasses on and walks over to the house with a backpack. She knocks on the door to see if anyone answers the door, no answer. She walks around to the side and through a gate to the back of the house. She checks the sliding glass door but that is locked.

She breaks a small area in a window and unlocks it and climbs through into the kitchen.

Once inside she slowly looks around at all the pictures with her parents and this innocent little girl. It's her. She walks through the house and comes to a little girl's bedroom. It has light tan colored walls, a bed with a pink bedspread, toys and stuffed animals are placed neatly on the bed. She also sees unwrapped gifts. Some say happy birthday and other say Merry Christmas on them. She thinks they must have still bought gifts for her, or this girl she doesn't know, waiting for her to return.

Tara goes into another room and sees stacks of flyers on a table and a map with different areas marked on it. Maybe this is where they looked or handed out flyers to find me, she thinks. She just thinks this is so sad and sick all at the same time. These people have wasted their lives looking, searching and nothing was ever found. They haven't really lived or enjoyed the life that was given to them. Tara walks up to the table and knocks off all the flyers from a pile, spilling them onto the floor. "Dumb Fucks." She whispers under her breath.

She goes out to the kitchen and makes herself something to eat while she waits for her parents to come home, or these people she doesn't even know. She turns on the TV and makes herself at home. Finally she hears a car door shut and keys jingle at the front door. Tara stands up and goes around the corner to wait for them to come in and shut the door. They see the TV is on and they just look at each other but before they can say a word Tara steps out in front of them, still with her wig and glasses on.

The man, her father asks in a loud voice, "Who are you? How did you get in here? What do you want?" He starts to lunge at her thinking she is just someone who broke into the house and was found by surprise. Tara quickly pulls out her gun from behind her and tells them both to sit the fuck down and shut up. Tara just stares at them for a while then asks them, "You don't know who I am?" She pulls off her wig and sunglasses. They see a young woman standing before them with long brown straight hair and piercing in her face. They just look confused and are not sure if they should speak or not, since Tara is holding them at gunpoint. Tara picks up a flyer and holds it next to her face from them to see. "It's me. I found my way back." Tara said to them. They both jump up and want to go to her. They tell her to put the gun down. "Its ok baby, it's me, your mother. I've never stopped looking for you." Her mother tells her while holding her arms out to Tara.

Tara yells at them to get in the kitchen and sit in the wooden chairs. Tara throws some rope at the man and tells him to tie up the woman. "Please Tammy, its ok, you don't have to be afraid anymore, you're home, you're safe!" The woman yells out. Tara then tells the man to sit down and Tara ties him to a kitchen chair too. Before they can get another word out, Tara grabs two small hand towels and shoves them in their mouths so they cannot speak anymore or yell. "Shut up!" Tara yells.

"Look at you two, wasted lives, you look horrible. You were looking for me? Well here I am. You like what you see? Was it all you had fucking hoped for? I've been watching you two for a couple weeks. You do nothing. You go to work and come home day in and day out like clock work. That is not living. Just existing as you breathe. And all those flyers! You needed to live! You could have lived for me! Instead you did nothing. Just hanging up flyers like you lost an old dog. I don't remember you. I don't know you! You're just fucking no good humans. I'm going to put you out of your misery, so you can be set free and start again! By the way, my name is fucking Tara, not Tammy." Tara says half yelling half talking. Tara has a silencer on her gun and just quickly shoots one bullet into each of their heads. They slump over in the chairs blood dripping out down both foreheads. Brains riddled all over the walls, window and the cabinets behind them.

Tara places her gun back in her holster, puts the wig and sunglasses back on and just walks out of the house leaving her parents dead bodies in the chairs across from each other. She quickly hops in her car and leaves. She takes off the wig and glasses a few blocks away and just chucks them out the window. She puts on her regular sunglasses, turns up the music and gets back on the highway headed east. Not wanting to waste anymore of her precious time on anything or anyone.

She does think of Mitch every now and again, sometimes she even thinks she sees her watching her, watching women, and she smiles. Tara just laughs. What is normal anyway? Mile after mile goes by as she drives not knowing where she will end up or who she will run into, a whole new world for Tara.

She still answers to Tara.

Printed in the United States of America

Normal as we Are

Author Desraye Halon

First Printing, 2014

Created 2008

RyBlu Publishing – Phoenix , AZ

Editing by D. S. C.

Photography for cover by Terese Halon Azad

For more information about the author go to

www.DesrayeHalonweebly.com

This book is dedicated to D. M. J.

Without you, this book would not have been possible. Thank you for everything, you will always be in our hearts.

THE END

Or is it………